MARIGOLD'S TALE

Be not forgetful to entertain strangers: for thereby some have entertained angels unawares

Hebrews 13:2

MARIGOLD'S TALE

BOOK TWO OF
THE LONELY ISLAND SERIES

MAGGIE ALLDER

Matador
Unit E2 Airfield Business Park,
Harrison Road, Market Harborough,
Leicestershire. LE16 7UL
Tel: 0116 2792299
Email: books@troubador.co.uk
Web: www.troubador.co.uk/matador
Twitter: @matadorbooks

ISBN 978 1803137 346

British Library Cataloguing in Publication Data.
A catalogue record for this book is available from the British Library.

Printed and bound in Great Britain by 4edge Limited
Typeset in 11pt Aldine401 BT by Troubador Publishing Ltd, Leicester, UK

Matador is an imprint of Troubador Publishing Ltd

To refugees everywhere,
and those who work with and for them.

ABOUT THE AUTHOR

Maggie Allder was born and brought up in Gamlingay in Cambridgeshire, the second daughter of a village police officer. She studied at King Alfred's College, Winchester (now the University of Winchester); in Richmond, Virginia; and later at the University of Reading. She taught for thirty-six years in a Hampshire comprehensive school. After exploring more orthodox forms of Christianity, Maggie became a Quaker and is happy and settled in the Quaker community in Winchester. She volunteers for a not-for-profit organisation, Human Writes, which aims to provide friendship to prisoners on death row in the United States.

Maggie has previously written three novels which form a trilogy of sorts: *Courting Rendition*, *Living with the Leopard* and *A Vision Softly Creeping*. Her fourth and fifth novels, *The Song of the Lost Boy* and *Beyond the Water Meadows*, each stand alone. All these first five novels take place in and around Winchester, UK. The first of the *Lonely Island* novels is called *Dark Waters*. *Marigold's Tale* is the second book in this series.

PROLOGUE

For the second time in a few months, a child was asleep on the settle in my bothy. This child, though, was at peace. She was warm and well, a slight smile on her face, the quilt drawn up to her shoulders, a slight flush on her cheeks.

Marigold.

It was her sister Lavender who had last lain there. Lavender, who had died in my arms just hours after I had found her on the beach. Lavender, who had started off the whole train of events that had led to the uncovering of a gang of arms smugglers and the release of a group of modern-day slaves who were climate refugees.

The child looked grubby, I thought. The whole group of refugees who had been tricked and abused by the smugglers had lived in the abandoned airport. I hadn't noticed when we were with them, but now, in my clean home, I could see it. Marigold's hair was lank, and she carried a slight aroma, of woodsmoke and sweat and of clothes washed only infrequently, and then not well.

Still, the sight of her lying there, warm and well fed and safe, made me smile. My own son, Duncan, used to take his afternoon naps on that settle when he was small, covered with that same quilt. It was good to have a child around.

The door of the bothy opened quietly and Malcolm came in. Briefly, through the open door, I saw the low afternoon sun and the darkening sea. Our island, En-Somi, is very far to the north – the sun sets early in the winter and rises late.

"Is she sleeping?" Malcolm asked, coming over to stand beside me, casually resting an arm around my waist. "She looks so young!"

"Nine is young!" I pointed out. "Can you remember being that age?"

Malcolm moved his arm and went over to the kitchen, in the south-western corner of the bothy, where our kitchens are traditionally always located. He filled the kettle and took out three mugs. "I was with Paps and Mam over on McGreggor Moor," he said. "At this time of year there wasn't too much to do other than tend the animals. We had a cow. My sister Moira used to milk her. My job was the chickens."

Just at that moment wee Marigold opened her eyes. For a moment she looked confused, then she turned her head, saw me and gave a huge grin. "I were asleep!" she remarked.

"Indeed, you were!" I agreed. "But don't worry, you didn't snore!"

The child frowned. "Is it bad to snore?" she wanted to know. "My dad snores. Is it rude?"

"*Nei, nei!*" Malcolm came over and looked down at the bairn. "Marie was teasing you. Would you like a cup of tea?"

Marigold sat up. "'Ave you got anything fizzy?" she wanted to know.

"Sorry, *nei*."

"Well, a cuppa will do!" the child conceded, and we all laughed.

CHAPTER 1

For the previous couple of days life had felt crazy; from the moment that the coastguard had arrived with two Shetland police officers, En-Somi had seemed incredibly busy. First the islanders and refugees, who were just about keeping the villains at bay and stopping them from making some sort of getaway, had been relieved. Then there were people talking on radios, islanders phoning friends and family, refugees distributing the unidentifiable soup and potatoes on which they seemed to live, and children running around, laughing, screaming and, inevitably, sometimes crying. Lyle, the local *nasyoni* or police officer, who had been involved with Malcolm, Verity (the minister of the kirk) and me in bringing down the smugglers, was talking to the Shetland officers and showing them the evidence which he had recorded on his phone. One of the coastguards, a kind-faced woman with an accent suggesting she had come originally from the Hebrides, was administering first aid, and more people were arriving from Storhaven because they had seen the helicopter landing and wanted to know what was going on. By lunchtime, two more helicopters had arrived. One carried more officials; the other brought reporters with cameras and microphones and accents that marked them, of course, as *un-fedii*, outsiders.

The crowds had dispersed only gradually, in dribs and drabs. Most of the refugees had gone back to the old airport where they had been squatting for ten years or so, although a few had remained around the elegant bothy where the villains had been caught. The people of Storhaven, the only settlement of any size on En-Somi, had mostly gone home. In the middle of the afternoon, before the sun had set, the largest of the three helicopters had taken off, carrying five men and a woman back to Lerwick where there were cells enough to hold them all. The two newspaper reporters and the very young-looking crew from BBC Alba, had wanted to know where the nearest hotel could be found and seemed to be rather put out to discover that there was no such establishment on the island. Once Ingrid and Dougie Fraser had offered them accommodation at their place, and they had left on foot in the gloomy late afternoon, there had only been the four of us, Marigold's family and two coastguards left.

"Better be getting back!" Si, Marigold's father, had remarked. He was holding their baby, Thistle, against his shoulder. He had sounded reluctant to leave.

"Suppose so," Rose, his wife, had agreed. "We don't want to miss no rations." She had sounded no more enthusiastic than her husband.

"Don't want to go back!" Marigold had announced, sounding more like a truculent teenager than a nine-year-old child. "I 'ates it there!"

"We all does," Si had sympathised. "But where else can we go?"

Lyle had been listening to the conversation. "I've got room at my place," he had offered. "It's a bit of a trek from here – I live over in Gamla Hus, but you'd be welcome…"

"Can we go in the cart?" Marigold had suddenly sounded excited again. "Wiv them ponies?"

Malcolm had laughed. "I think you'll have to!" he had answered. "It's too far for walking, after everything we've been through today!"

So it was that the first of the refugees had left the old airport.

★★★

2

Although the island is so remote, our internet connections remain sound unless the weather turns against us. It was strange, that evening, watching the television reports of things with which we had been so closely involved. There was an aerial shot of the island, making it look so small and desolate. I realised all over again why it is called En-Somi, the Lonely Island. There was some film of one of the reporters standing with his back to the Storhaven harbour, talking to the camera about arms smugglers and climate refugees and how all this had been happening on an island where the only reported crime in the previous twelve months had been three cases of drunk-and-disorderly and a dispute over land ownership that had led to a fight and a broken jaw. Those of us directly involved in the events of the last few weeks had been advised by the Shetland police officers not to talk to the press, but there were a few seconds of film showing Marigold's family, Malcolm, Lyle and me climbing onto Malcolm's cart and heading off down the track on our way back to Hus. There was some talk of a 'simple community' where people still had a subsistence economy and where there were no motorised vehicles. There was no mention of the fact that we were carbon neutral, that we produced our own power and that our average life expectancy was three years longer than on the mainland.

Once we had dropped Lyle and Marigold's family over at Lyle's bothy in Gamla Hus, Malcolm had driven his cart down the rugged track to his bothy. From there it is a good twenty minutes of hard walking to my place and it was not an inviting prospect to set out again, so we opened a new bottle of whisky, Malcolm broke a few eggs into a pan and cut some thick slices of wholemeal bread, and I stayed the night.

★★★

It's all a long time ago now, but I recall some of what followed with crystal clarity. I suppose that we were all bound to dwell on events that were so out of the ordinary, although nowadays, sitting by the fire in the *fi'ilsted* (the pub), it's surprising how those of us who were involved at the time remember different things, or remember the same things differently.

For example, how did it come about that so many of the refugees came to live on the west of the island, in and around our village? Of course, Lyle had offered his home to Si, Rose and their two children on that first day, so it wasn't surprising that they stayed. It was a pretty impractical arrangement, though. Most of our homes are very simple. Over in Storhaven, the little harbour town in the east where the ferry comes in, houses are divided into rooms and although most were originally single-story buildings, many families have extended into their attics. Out here in the moorland, though, our homes tend to be very traditional. Lyle had one large room and a stone addition which served as his office and where they set up beds for Marigold's family, but it was crowded and if anyone needed the bathroom in the night they had to pass through the main room where Lyle slept. In the daytime, too, whenever anyone came to talk *nasyoni* business with Lyle, all his guests needed to get out of the way. That arrangement lasted for a bit less than a fortnight before the little family gravitated to the *fi'ilsted* for most of their daytime activities.

In fact, now that I think about it, it was the very next day that Marigold turned up at my place. Malcolm and I had slept late. I remember Malcolm bringing me a cup of tea, nudging my shoulder, offering me porridge with island honey on it, well after 11.00 am. I had dumped my backpack in the corner of the bothy when we came in the evening before, but everything in it was dirty. We had been camping out, living rough, for several days before the coastguard had rescued us. I had slept in an old shirt of Malcolm's and was still pottering about dressed like that as we planned what was left of our day.

"You can stay here," Malcolm said, "as long as you want. You know that, don't you?"

Of course, I did. We had been getting gradually closer ever since we had met in the village shop in the autumn. Being with Malcolm seemed like an entirely natural thing, unremarkable, as if we had always been together. On the other hand, I had a bothy of my own to tend to.

"I really ought to check on my chickens!" I said. It seemed as if I'd been thinking of nothing but those chickens wherever I had been over the previous few days!

We both laughed. "I'll walk over with you," offered Malcolm. "Just let me put some clothes in the machine. Do you think my sleeping bag will be machine-washable too? It's filthy!"

"Bound to be," I reassured him. "I'll need to do the same when I get home."

I remember that it was an unusually calm day. It is almost always windy on En-Somi, and Malcolm's bothy, like mine, seems to be perched on the edge of the island, facing a deep drop and miles of sea. There was a low, hazy sun, but the air was cold. We pulled our quilted hoods up and followed the burn north. We didn't talk much. It's one of the things I've always loved about being with Malcolm. When we're in the mood we can talk for hours, but silence between us is a comfortable thing, made of understanding and peace.

I had a sore foot and I remember that I felt stiff all over. There is one place, on the walk between Malcolm's home and mine, where you have to climb over a stone wall. It had never, once, been a problem for me until that day. We both laughed as Malcolm helped me over, and said that this was what it would be like when we got old. Malcolm started humming an old Beatles song about still loving each other when we were sixty-four. We were still chuckling as we came over the hill to my bothy, and there was Marigold.

"Good heavens!" exclaimed Malcolm. "How did you get here?"

Marigold looked a little wary. "Followed a track!" she told us.

5

"*Aja*, but…" I knew that Marigold had never been to this side of the island until she arrived in Malcolm's pony-drawn cart the evening before.

"Lyle told me 'ow to find you," the bairn explained. "I fought what I would come and see you."

"Well, I'm glad you did!" I said, opening the door. "Come in. Are you hungry? Did Lyle give you lunch?"

She followed me in, looking around the one room of the bothy, walking over to the west-facing window and looking out, touching the rough stone wall and the smooth, polished wood of the rocking chairs.

"Is this your 'ome, then?" she wondered. "Just this one room?"

Malcolm was in then, too, and had closed the door. "Cosy, isn't it?" he remarked.

"Ye – es…" I could tell that Marigold was unsure. "I fought what you would 'ave lots of rooms, like that 'ouse what them bosses lived in. Lyle, 'e's only got one room too, and a' office. We slept in the office."

The child walked over to the stepladder which leads up to my sleeping platform. "What's up 'ere?" she wanted to know. "Is you poor? I fought that only poor people 'ad to live all in one room?" Then she looked at the shelves which my husband Bjorn had built years ago, along the eastern wall of the bothy. "All them books!" remarked Marigold. "You don't seem like no poor person to me!"

I laughed. "I'm not poor," I explained. "I have everything I need here. Why would I want anything more?"

Marigold had found a photo of my son Duncan in his school uniform, taken the previous summer just before he had gone to Shetland to school. "'O is this?" she wanted to know.

"My son."

She wrinkled up her nose. "Oh, yeah… you told me. The boy with the boss name. Duncan?"

"Well remembered!" I congratulated her. "I'll tell you what, Marigold. I need to check that my chickens are all right, then I'll make a drink. Could you eat a biscuit or two? Would you like to come and help me?"

But the child had plonked herself down on the settle. "Can I just stay 'ere?" she asked. "I's a bit tired."

"Of course," I agreed and fetched the quilt. "I won't be a minute."

"I'll come with you," Malcolm said to me.

We were probably only out of the bothy for ten or fifteen minutes – as long as it took to top up the chicken's food and water, to check the temperature of their coop and to gather up the three eggs that had been laid in my absence. Then Malcolm climbed the slope behind the bothy to check the wind turbine, and I went back inside.

And found Marigold fast asleep.

CHAPTER 2

With the weather calm like that, my phone reception was good. I phoned Lyle while Malcolm made the tea and rooted out the biscuits. I explained that Marigold was with us, and that she was staying for some tea. In the background I could hear Thistle crying.

"How's it going?" I asked.

Lyle chuckled. "I always thought I wanted bairns," he told me, "but I'm not so sure now. Wee Thistle's been crying all day. And I was woken four times last night by young Marigold wandering through to the bathroom. I don't think that child ever sleeps!"

"Oh, *aja*, she does!" I assured him. "She's done nothing else since we found her here this afternoon!"

"Oh dear!" Lyle sounded remorseful. "Did you mind me telling her how to find your place? She was so keen to see you, and there was nothing for her to do here…"

"*Nei*, that's fine!" I reassured him.

Then I had an idea. "Can I talk to Si or Rose?" I wondered.

Lyle passed the phone to Rose. For a moment all I could hear was Thistle's wailing, then Rose saying, "'Ere, Si, well you take 'er?" Then, "'Ello, Marie. Is she being a problem, our Marigold?"

"*Nei, nei*! Quite the opposite," I told her. "She's the perfect guest. But it'll get dark soon, and she shouldn't walk home on her own on a track she doesn't know. I wondered if you'd let her stay here for the night? I've got a spare bed while Duncan's away at school…"

I thought I heard a sigh of relief. "If you're sure it's no bother?" Poor Rose sounded at her wits' end. "She really didn't settle last night. I fink Lyle got a bit fed up…"

I could hear Lyle in the background. "*Nei*, I didn't! I love having you here!"

I chuckled. "Let me just check with Marigold," I suggested. "I'm thinking she's never spent a night away from you before?"

★★★

But Marigold jumped at the idea. "Will I sleep 'ere?" she wanted to know, pointing at the settle. So I showed her Duncan's bed in a cupboard-like alcove at the other end of the room and introduced her to the bathroom.

Marigold stood at the door of the elegant Scandinavian-style wet room and gave a deep sigh. "Now I knows you is rich!" she proclaimed. "Can I 'ave a shower? I ain't never 'ad one. Mum and Dad, they 'ad showers back before we was brought to this 'ere island, but us kids, what was born 'ere…"

"Of course you can!" I agreed. "And I'll see if I have any of Duncan's clothes left – any that will fit you. Then we can wash what you're wearing now."

"Where'll you sleep?" was her next question.

"My bed is up on that platform," I explained, pointing to the ladder. "I won't be far away, if you want me in the night. We'll be in the same room, really."

"And 'im?" The child jerked her thumb over her shoulder towards Malcolm, who was sitting in a rocking chair nursing his mug of tea.

"I'll sleep up there too," he answered. "If that's all right with Marie?"

"Of course," I agreed. "So, perhaps we ought to think about dinner?"

The child was interested in everything we did. It was as if she were visiting a different country – or a different period in history. Malcolm set about cooking a chicken pie, defrosting some chicken from my freezer and making the pastry from scratch. That in itself was a cause of fascination to Marigold.

"We 'ad chicken once," she told us. "Jarvis stole it from somewhere and we 'ad to 'ide the feavers in case the bosses found out we was stealing. But there weren't much meat and it tasted odd."

She was amazed at the range I cook on. It is, of course, heated by electricity harvested by my turbine but designed to look like an old-fashioned range with a panel that glows in a very lifelike way. Marigold frowned at it for a minute or two and then wanted to know, "Where's the smoke?" I realised that she thought I had real solid fuel burning there, and that perhaps she had never seen anyone cooking over anything other than an open fire.

"I'll explain that to you later," promised Malcolm. "If you want to have a shower in Marie's posh bathroom, you probably ought to take it now. This pie'll take half an hour to bake, once I put it in the oven."

"Oven," repeated Marigold, savouring a new word, then followed me as I rooted through what was left of Duncan's cast-offs.

We didn't do too well on the clothes' front. I had already taken quite a lot of the things Duncan had outgrown over to the old airport where the refugees had been squatting, and Marigold was extremely assertive about what she would wear. "I ain't dressing in no boy's cloves!" she insisted.

In the end we found her a pair of jeans which were acceptable (if long) and a *gensi* of mine which she wore like a tunic, then we proceeded to the shower, which was quite a business in itself. Marigold loved the warm water and was fascinated with the bubbles made by the shampoo. I think she would have stayed there for hours, but Malcolm called out, "Dinner in five minutes!" so I wrapped the child in one of my big, fleecy bath towels and left her to dress, while I set the table.

The washing machine was the next exciting adventure to be encountered that evening. Over at the old airport the refugees had washed their clothes by hand in cold water. They had not had any choice. Marigold stared in fascination at the circular window of the machine, as the clothes and my sleeping bag churned round and round. "Where does the water go?" she wanted to know and wasn't satisfied until Malcolm took a piece of paper and drew a diagram showing the way the water got into the machine and where it went afterwards. "You've got it all sussed!" was the child's approving comment.

I gave her an old T-shirt to sleep in, although the idea of taking off your clothes to go to bed was a novelty for the child. "I'll get cold!" she worried, eyeing the pink garment with a butterfly design on the front rather warily.

"*Nei*, you won't," I reassured her. "Look, all these covers will be on top of you, and if you feel the wall by your feet, you'll see that it's warm. Duncan was never cold in bed."

She touched the wall, which has the hot water tank in the chimney behind it, and seemed satisfied. Then she snuggled down under the winter duvet and patchwork quilt and gave a little sigh of contentment. "I bet Duncan misses 'is bed!" she murmured and was asleep before I walked softly away.

★★★

It was not to be expected that, having taken initial statements from us the day before, the Shetland police would leave us alone. We were still having breakfast, the three of us, when Lyle phoned the next day.

"They want to check out some more details with you," he explained, "and the BBC Alba people have come over from Storhaven and want to interview you too, about life on the island. Apparently, that's acceptable, as long as you don't talk about the case we're dealing with. Petter and Malchi are offering everyone lunch at the *fi'ilsted*. But of course, that bit's up to you."

I took Marigold out to see if the hens had laid. She was a bit nervous of them but interested in the way they were fed and watered, and delighted by my tale of birds being blown away when Bjorn and I had first started keeping chickens and hadn't realised how vulnerable they would be in the strong Atlantic gales. I showed her the little, walled area where I grew kale, sheltered from the insistent En-Somi winds, and we talked about the south-facing slopes where some people grew oats, though my land didn't lend itself to such a crop. She stood on the flat area in front of my bothy, looking out towards the wild ocean. She sniffed the air. "You can't smell no smoke," said the child who had spent the first nine years of her life by a campfire. "Just... air! You can smell air 'ere!"

I laughed. "In a way," I agreed. "And plants. And the sea. Look, I have thistles growing here. Just like the ones where you used to live."

She turned to look at me then. "I miss Thistle," she said, rather sadly.

"Don't worry," I reassured her. "We'll go back up to the village soon, when Malcolm has gone home to his place. He'll meet us in the village."

The child cheered up at once. "Will 'e 'ave 'is ponies?" she wanted to know, and skipped inside to check that detail with Malcolm.

★★★

There are only two proper settlements on En-Somi. Storhaven is called a town but in most other places people would say it was a village. Our village, Gamla Hus, was even smaller then than it is now, and consisted of a school (two rooms), the *fi'ilsted*, the shop and a few bothies. Since there have never been motorised vehicles on the island the roads are not paved, but two tracks cross by the village shop, and people come in from the outlying bothies on the moors. The *fi'ilsted* was the centre of social life for all of us who lived in the west of the island – to a large extent it still is.

Marigold and I left my bothy at the same time as Malcolm, although of course we were heading in different directions. The child watched approvingly as Malcolm kissed me goodbye. "I knew 'e were your bloke," she commented, tucking her hand into mine, "even though you said 'e were just a friend!"

The village was remarkably busy. The BBC Alba people had borrowed a cart from someone over in Storhaven, and their ponies were tethered outside the *fi'ilsted*. Several families had come in from the surrounding hillsides to talk about everything that had happened, and people were coming in and out of the school where the Shetland police were interviewing people. There was a general air of excitement, like the days leading up to an island festival.

Marigold and I went to Lyle's bothy first. He wasn't there, but Rose was sitting by the fire and Thistle was sleeping in a makeshift cradle made from one of the drawers of Lyle's chest-of-drawers. She looked up as we came in.

"Marigold!" Rose exclaimed, surprised. Then she looked at me. "She looks so different!" she added.

It was true. I had put the child's hair in a ponytail high on the back of her head, the way many of the village children, boys and girls, wear their hair. The *gensi*, or knitted pullover, which had once been mine, was made of bright greens and blues against a background of natural cream wool, and the jeans were a deep blue too. The refugees always seemed to be dressed in shades of grey and brown – Rose herself was still wearing the outfit I had always seen her in at the old airport. By contrast, Marigold looked young and bright and clean. You could have mistaken her for one of the village children until she opened her mouth.

"'Ello, Mum!" she said, skipping into the room and going over at once to look at baby Thistle. "'As she been good?" she wanted to know. Then, "Marie's got a machine what washes cloves and a thing what cooks food – a' oven." She was showing off her new word. "And I 'ad a shower wiv 'ot water, and I've got new cloves!"

Rose looked at me, a worried expression on her face.

"'Ello, love!" she answered. "Will you go and find your dad? I fink 'e's at that pub up the track. 'E'll be pleased to see you, looking so posh!" Her eyes followed her daughter as the wee bairn skipped out, full of confidence. Then, when the child had left, she told me what was on her mind. "Marie, you bin good to us, and I's grateful, but I's worried if you's spoiling that child. We don't know what'll 'appen to us now. Could be we'll 'ave to leave this 'ere island and go to another camp… She ain't gonna 'ave a life like yours, that one. Best not to give 'er too many ideas."

"Oh, Rose!" I felt so sorry. "I didn't mean… but do you want to leave the island? I mean… wasn't Marigold born here? This is her home!"

Rose sighed. "I don't fink you understand," she commented. "People like us, we don't 'ave no 'ome."

CHAPTER 3

The police officers, when they interviewed me again, were kind but not a bit like the Edinburgh or London police you see on television. For one thing, they were clearly fascinated with the whole story of the way we had discovered, step by step, what was going on in and around the old airport: the holding of the climate refugees as slaves, the assembling of drone weapons and the way they were smuggled away from the island. Talking to them was much more like telling a story in the *fi'ilsted* than making a formal statement, and at one point I noticed that the younger of the two officers was even sitting forward in his chair, as if on tenterhooks, to hear what would happen next. Then, too, we use dialect words on En-Somi which are not used anywhere else. I wasn't born on the island, and I can only say the most elementary things in the local tongue, but some words, like *'harkrav'*, are in everyday use, and there is really no satisfactory English word expressing the same concept. It means something like, 'the entitled ones' or 'the landed class'. In a way, the refugees had the best translation when they just called the *harkrav* 'the bosses'.

Anyhow, each time I used one of these dialect words, the older of the two officers stopped me to clarify my meaning, although by then he had been on the island for almost twenty-four hours and must have heard those words dozens of times. They recorded my statement on a machine which then printed it off automatically, but the machine couldn't spell En-Somi dialect, so the print-offs were rather amusing and had to be corrected. Both officers seemed quite light-hearted about the whole business.

"We've already got all the evidence we need!" the older man explained. "This is a real open-and-shut case."

"And we've been offered lunch at that pub of yours," added the other. "The police aren't always treated as well as this, you can take our word for it!"

★★★

The *fi'ilsted* was as crowded as I had ever seen it. Si, Rose and Marigold were sitting in the corner beneath the sepia photos of local people 150 years earlier. They were eating fish stew and dumplings. Thistle was asleep in a sling which Rose was wearing. The Kullanders had come down from their place. Alf and Fiona were sitting by the fire talking to Jamie MacLoughlan, who hadn't been involved in the recent adventures. Olaf was sitting in the north-eastern corner away from the fire, a far-away look on his face, his *langspil* in its case beside him. I guessed that he was composing a ballad to record the events of the winter. If you've seen the documentary that the BBC Alba people made about the island, you'll have heard that ballad. It's the wild, wandering song he sings as the titles go up at the end. Most of the people from the outlying bothies were there, although Marigold and Thistle were the only wee ones inside. The shouts and cheers that came from the track outside told the tale of an impromptu football match involving most of the other bairns. School, of course, was closed, so that the Shetland *nasyonii* could use the only building of any size for interviews.

I went over to greet Si and Rose. "Enjoying Malchi's food?" I asked. It was, by common agreement, the best food on the island.

"It's *fish*!" exclaimed Marigold, looking indignant. "Fish!"

I was slightly taken aback. We eat a lot of fish on En-Somi, which is not surprising given that we have been allocated a generous fishing quota and are surrounded by the wild North Atlantic.

"I told you," Si said to his daughter, "all sorts of people eats fish."

Rose looked at me apologetically. "She thinks it's refugee food," she explained. "We caught quite a lot over at the camp. Because we never really 'ad meat."

"I love fish!" I commented. "And Malchi makes the best fish stew for hundreds of miles!"

"Probably for thousands of miles!" suggested Malcolm, coming up behind me.

Marigold looked from one to the other of us. "It's all right," she conceded. "But last night you made chicken pie! In a' oven."

Malcolm laughed. "And I'll cook you lamb chops later this year!" he promised.

Rose dropped her spoon with a clatter onto her empty dish. She was frowning. "Time we was back at Lyle's!" she demanded.

"But Mum…!"

Si was looking at Rose with one eyebrow raised. He wasn't sure what was going on, but he backed her up. "Good idea," he agreed, lifting his bowl to his lips and drinking the last of his stew without the need of his spoon. "I wants to look at the way Lyle stores 'is spuds."

Petter came over to clear the table. "They left in a hurry," he commented.

"Did they pay?" Malcolm asked. "I don't suppose they've got any money. Put it on my tab."

Petter straightened up and gave Malcolm one of his direct looks. "I know this is a business," he said, "but you've been here long enough, and you're no *un-fed*! Do you really think I'd withhold food from the hungry just because they couldn't pay?"

I saw by the dim light in the *fi'ilsted* that Malcolm had gone red. "*Nei*, of course not!" he answered. "Sorry."

Petter smiled a forgiving smile. "So why did they leave at such speed?" he wanted to know.

"Good question." Malcolm was looking concerned.

I thought I'd better explain. "I think it's because Malcolm said he'll cook lamb chops for Marigold later in the year. Rose thinks they'll be taken off the island now, that they'll be sent to another camp. She doesn't want Marigold settling in with us and then being uprooted again."

Petter put the dirty dishes back on the table and looked between Malcolm and me. "But that can't happen!" he exclaimed. "Surely... I mean... would the authorities do that?"

Malcolm answered rather grimly, "Ten years ago the authorities brought a crowd of climate refugees up here and housed them in tents by the runway of the old airport. Tents! In this climate! Refugees from south of the border, with no skills at all to help them to survive up here! So, it doesn't seem so improbable to me that they'd ship that little family and their friends off somewhere else! And I can't see the *Oyrod*, the island council, wanting them here, can you? Refugees cost money. Nobody really wants them, you know that!"

Petter looked up at the old sepia photos on the wall, then back at us. "You might be right," he said, thoughtfully. "The island council is fine when it comes to the ordinary, everyday running of En-Somi, but I'm not sure I'd trust them with questions of principle. They're too concerned about their wallets."

"*Aja,*" agreed Malcolm. "Too many *harkrav* on the council, not enough people who understand how life feels for ordinary people." He sighed. "It was just the same when I worked in Edinburgh. You wouldn't believe the number of good schemes that failed because of a lack of proper investment."

Petter picked up the dirty dishes again. "Perhaps it's time we took matters into our own hands?" he suggested and went off to the kitchen without waiting for a reply.

★★★

18

We knew that the police had finished taking statements when they arrived at the *fi'ilsted*, laughing at something that the village schoolteacher, Sigrid, was saying. They stopped just inside the low-ceilinged room and looked around.

"Grand!" approved the older officer, taking off his cap.

"Something smells good," remarked the other.

Petter came out from behind the bar. "Malchi's made fish stew and dumplings today," he told the men. "There's room for you there, in the corner. You know Marie and Malcolm, obviously. Would you take a whisky now, if you're off duty?"

The two men joined us at the table where Marigold's family had been sitting.

"This place reminds me of that place on Easdale," remarked the older officer. "Have you been there? It's another island, like yours, with no cars…"

"No arms smugglers, either!" laughed the younger officer. "I'm Gordon. No need to call me 'officer' now!"

"They call me MacDuff," added the older officer.

"He's called Ian, really," Gordon added, "but he comes from Fife, and he fights for law and order. So, MacDuff. Just like in Shakespeare!"

We all laughed then, and Petter brought over four dishes of steaming fish stew, then went back for a tray of drinks.

"We were talking about the refugees," explained Malcolm after a spoonful or two of his food. "Do you know what'll happen to them now?"

"Hard to say," answered MacDuff. "It's a bit of an embarrassment, I would say, for the bigwigs in Edinburgh. How could it happen that a group of refugees was left behind all this time? There've been questions in Holyrood already, and the Home Secretary down in London is busy blaming the Scottish authorities… So, does that Malchi do all the cooking here? He could make a fortune on the mainland!"

"He would never leave the island," answered Malcolm. "So

do you think they'll send them to a new camp, the refugees?"

"Probably," said Gordon. "Poor things!"

"But couldn't we stop them?" Malcolm persisted. "What if they want to stay here?"

"Not really my area of expertise," frowned MacDuff. "We're just police. You ought to talk to those reporter laddies. They'll know about this sort of thing. Good whisky, by the way! Is it distilled here?"

★★★

The BBC Alba crew were also eating in the *fi'ilsted*. Well, of course, there was nowhere else to buy food, unless they wanted expensive, imported chocolate bars from the shop! There were three of them. At first, when Malcolm and I went over to them, I thought it was three young men, not much more than students by the look of them, but as we started talking, I realised that one was a woman – a lassie, really. She was wearing one of those wide, floppy berets that folk singers in those days used to wear. Unlike virtually everyone else in the room, she was eating bread and goat's cheese, with some of Malchi's amazing kale chutney. "I don't like fish," she remarked, pulling a face.

We explained our question: was there any way they could suggest of keeping the refugees on the island – if, in fact, they wanted to stay?

"Sorry," it was one of the young men who answered. "It's not the sort of thing we'd know. We're doing our work experience placement with Alba; we're not really proper professional reporters yet!"

"But it would make a good story!" suggested the girl. "If a lot of islanders want them to stay – and if the refugees want to stay!"

Which set Malcolm and me thinking even more.

★★★

Verity came over that afternoon. She looked tired and unhappy. We had all finished eating, and Olaf was singing his 'Ballad of the *Huldufolk*' which he had composed in the autumn. The BBC Alba people had migrated to his corner of the *fi'ilsted* and were recording the music, their eyes shining. There were too many people there for everyone to sit on chairs – the tables had been pushed back against the walls and were being used as extra seating, and the bairns who had come in from their football game were sitting on laps or cross-legged on the floor. I saw young Elin sitting on the slates at Olaf's feet. She was a wee one then but already fascinated by the old ways. Who would have guessed that she would become the next bard of the island, the first woman to have that role?

Lyle and Verity came over to our corner and squeezed themselves onto the table where we were then perched. Malchi was sitting on a stool at our feet with a tray on his lap, finishing his meal. Of course, he hadn't started eating until everyone else was served.

Malcolm reached out and touched Verity's hand. "How're things over in Storhaven?" he wanted to know.

Verity sighed. "Strange," was her answer. "The whole town seems to be taking sides. Some people are excited because we're on the news; others think we've brought the island into disrepute. I went to the Copper Kettle for breakfast this morning. It was full of people arguing. Some folk think the whole thing should've been hushed up – the refugees don't belong here, but Fox-Drummin and his crowd do. They've done a lot for the island. Now they've been arrested and taken away to stand trial, while the town has been inundated with refugees. Charlie and Shawn from out at the old airport came in when I was just finishing my meal, and went from table to table begging. People say there've never been beggars on En-Somi before!"

"Why were they begging?" I asked, and then answered my own question as realisation dawned. "They were given their food, such as it was, by their bosses. Now that the bosses have been taken off the island, there isn't anyone to give them food."

"Yes," agreed Verity. "And the other thing is, that with Sergeant Stensen arrested, there's nobody over on the east of the island to calm things down. I heard that there was a fight of sorts outside the Old Castle *fi'ilsted*, when two *harkrav* men started blaming young Harris for stirring up trouble with the coastguard. Well, you know Harris – he won't stand being patronised by *harkrav*!"

Malcolm was looking worried. There was a pause in the music, so Malchi heard him say, "So haven't the authorities put anything in place for the people out at the old airport?"

Malchi turned round and looked up at us all. "They'll do nothing," he said. "They'll pass the problem to the *Oyrod*. Remember, I was a refugee myself – well, an asylum seeker actually, I've seen how the system works – or doesn't work. If the people in Storhaven make enough fuss, I'm sure they'll move the refugees on, but they'll just dump them somewhere else. At least, because they're climate refugees, they'll get to stay in the country. I was lucky not to be sent back where I came from – which would've been certain death."

Lyle asked Verity, "What do you think the mood is, in Storhaven? Do you think most people want the refugees to go?"

Verity looked thoughtful. Then, "Well, you know I haven't been here for long, but I'd say that most of the *bondii* (she meant the ordinary people) would be quite happy if the refugees stayed, as long as they were settled somewhere. They don't approve of the begging, though. But the island council is made up mostly of *harkrav*, and they won't like the fact that Fox-Drummin and his crowd have been caught out. And after only a few months I already know that the *harkrav* are not known for their soft hearts! And I don't understand it, but there are some ordinary people who still support the five who were arrested, even though we all know now that they're criminals." She wrinkled up her nose. "The *harkrav* seem to think that the law doesn't apply to them, and some of the *bondii* seem to agree."

"It's what we're used to," Lyle commented. "The *harkrav* have always taken the lead, and the island has prospered, well enough. And people don't like change."

"But we're talking about criminal activities!" Verity was indignant.

"*Aja*," Lyle agreed. "But nothing that hurt us…"

"Then it's time for action!" announced Malcolm, sounding suddenly very resolute.

★★★

Just at that moment Patrick and Shona came in. They ran the shop back in those days, so their work had kept them away from the feast at the *fi'ilsted*. They made their way through the crowd to our corner.

"*Hei!*" they greeted us. Then Shona addressed Lyle. "We've had an idea," she said.

Lyle was looking worried. The rest of us were all just ordinary *bondii*, perhaps you might call us peasants, but he was one of the few people on En-Somi with official responsibility. And, what was more, with his sergeant under arrest, he was the only representative of law and order on En-Somi.

"How can I help?" he asked, looking concerned. I suppose that people had been in and out of his crowded bothy all morning with queries, suggestions and gossip.

"Well," explained Patrick, "actually, we think we might be able to help you."

Just then Olaf started to sing an ancient fishing ballad, the song that tells of the wreck of the *Sea Maiden* by the Stacks of Seamus and the miraculous rescue of all those on board. The noise in the room dropped as the tale was sung, parents rocking their young ones to the rhythm of the music, children mouthing the words that they were still learning.

Shona almost whispered, so as not to disturb the

23

atmosphere. "We were wondering about the bothy up the track from us – we thought that wee family you are housing could live there."

I felt Malcolm grasp my hand. He was excited. "Well, that would be a start!" he hissed.

There was a stillness when Olaf had played his last note. Why is it that the music of the island is so often sad, and yet, without fail, it leaves me feeling happy and deeply connected to everyone else? It was the ideal moment for Malcolm.

"*En-Som-in-Fedii*!" he called, standing, moving into the small space in front of Malchi. "Fellow islanders! I want to propose a toast. To Petter and Malchi, for this wonderful meal!"

All round the *fi'ilsted* glasses were raised.

"*Shlainte*!"

"Cheers!"

"To Petter and Malchi!"

"To fish stew!"

People were laughing. Malcolm had tapped into everyone's sense of well-being.

"We are a fortunate people," Malcolm went on. "We have this island, we have each other, we have everything we need for a good life!"

"Except sunshine!" called out someone, and there was a general ripple of laughter.

Malcolm grinned at the interruption and then continued. "But now there are those among us who have nothing." He looked serious again. "Back at Lyle's there's a little family who have nowhere to go. There are two children who were born here on En-Somi, who could be sent away at any time, to who-knows-where. And over in Storhaven there are more – men, women and children who were kept as slaves – *slaves* – here on this lonely island of ours. And are we content for them just to be sent away? Is that what we are like?"

There were murmurs from around the room. Someone said,

"But what can we do?" and another voice asked, "Are they even honest? Can we trust them?"

Then Shona spoke up. "There's lots we could do," she called out. "To begin with, we could help the family Malcolm spoke about, the people in Lyle's cottage."

"How?"

"What're you thinking?"

"With what?"

Patrick spoke up at that point. "Just up the track from our shop," he reminded everyone, "there are two ruined bothies. Why don't we renovate one of them? That would be a start!"

There was a buzz of conversation. People were talking to those sitting or standing next to them, weighing up the possibilities.

Sigrid spoke up, "There's room for more children in the school," she pointed out. "They'll want to close us if we fall below ten bairns, so a few more families would be a good thing!"

"There are no permissions on those properties," pointed out Yanni Sinclair. It had taken their family a little over two years before the authorities had granted them a licence for their wind turbine. The frustration was still fresh in his mind.

"And there's no piped water either," Alf Kullander added. "My paps used to tell me about old Buck Stewart collecting his water from the burn."

"That's true," agreed Paula Stewart. "He was Robbie's great-uncle. And he lived to be eighty-something, so there can't have been much wrong with the water!"

"We make enough electricity for two households," Patrick told us. "We could rig something up for the time being – until they have their own turbine."

"It would cost a pretty penny!" commented Jamie MacLoughlan.

"I've got savings," offered Malchi. "I'd like to help. You all made me so welcome when I first arrived…"

"We could do a lot of the work ourselves," suggested Robert.

"Lyle needs his space," put in Shona.

And so it was agreed.

★★★

I wasn't there when Lyle and Verity told Si and Rose about the suggestion of the *bondii* of Gamla Hus, that we renovate a bothy for them. I was still at the *fï'ilsted*, where there was a general air of excitement. To be honest, I'm not sure the idea would have caught on so quickly if Malcolm had made the same suggestion in the summer, when everyone is so busy, but February is a dark, empty month. New boats have been built and old boats mended. There is little farming to be done – we plant our potatoes in April and those who grow spring oats start a little earlier than that, perhaps mid-March, depending on the weather. There is almost no fishing. The men, especially, would be grateful for a project that would bring them all together.

I was talking to Petter and Alf about how to apply for the necessary licences. The two bothies up the track above the shop, the track that leads to the Fyrtarn Fjell pass, had both been in ruins for forty or more years, and nobody was quite sure who owned them. Shona stabled her goats in the one closest to their bothy, but she was happy enough to move them out now that Patrick had promised to build her stabling just up from the marsh over towards the field Sigrid used.

"Maybe nobody owns the ruins now?" wondered Alf.

"I think it's Stewart property," Petter guessed. "Buck Stewart was the last one to live there. So, if Robbie and Paula don't mind, I can't think anyone else will."

We were all sitting around, discussing the pros and cons of doing the renovation while Malchi and Petter sorted out the *fï'ilsted*, when Marigold reappeared. Most of the families from the outlying bothies had returned home, and Robert had taken the BBC Alba people down to the summer harbour. It was about

4.00 pm, I suppose, still light, but shadowy because the village is in the valley, and Fyrtarn Fjell blocks the late afternoon sun. Marigold stood in the open door looking around, then she saw me and ran across the slate flags.

"Marie!" she exclaimed, almost throwing herself at me. "Marie! They says what we can stay. 'Ere! In this… this… this place!"

I laughed. "We hope so," I agreed, holding the child, who was quivering with excitement. "It's partly up to your mam and paps."

She giggled. "Not 'mam and paps'!" she corrected me. "Mum and dad! And they wants to stay! I 'eard 'em telling that vicar lady. They said 'ere is as good as anywhere, and better than most. So will Malcolm make me that lamb… them lamb… them fings what 'e said 'e'd cook for me?"

Everyone was laughing. "Lamb chops," said Malcolm. "I'll cook them for your whole family, the day we move you into your new bothy."

"Not that his cooking's as good as Malchi's," said Petter, who was sweeping dumpling crumbs up off the floor.

Marigold suddenly looked serious, almost worried. "Malcolm," she explained, "Thistle can't eat no lamb anyfings. She's still a baby!"

"No problem," Malcolm reassured her. "I'll eat Thistle's!"

★★★

There was a spell of five calm days following our decision to renovate the Stewart bothy, which was unusual but extremely convenient. We all asked around, but nobody knew whose land the two ruined buildings occupied, and any deeds that might exist would probably be held in Edinburgh. Lyle and Malcolm sent off emails to everyone they could think of who might be able to trace the owners, but in the meantime Robert, Alf Kullander (aided by his son Andy) and Petter, when he wasn't serving customers at the *fi'ilsted*, were engaged in some preliminary demolition. The western wall of the bothy was in very poor condition, being the most exposed to the weather, and they took it down, stone by stone, and rebuilt it. Patrick rushed around like crazy, finishing the stabling for Shona's goats, which he had been promising her (she said) for years. The floor of the bothy was made of slate, and when the right permissions had been gained, underfloor heating would be installed. That meant that the floor had to be lifted and the slates stacked carefully ready to be re-used, but nothing could be done until we knew who the land belonged to. For the time being, Si, Rose and the children still slept at Lyle's, but since Petter and Malchi had more or less taken over the responsibility of feeding them, Lyle seemed to be coping better.

Verity had returned almost at once to Storhaven. As the minister of the kirk, she felt that she needed to be there. Her congregation was unhappy, divided between those who thought she was in the wrong because of her part in bringing Fox-Drummin and his sidekick, Duncan, to justice, when they had hitherto been considered such upright members of the community, and those who felt that she had done entirely the right thing.

★★★

Malcolm and I were in the shop a few days later when Lyle came in. We had ordered new clothes for the little family, via the internet. They would arrive by ferry to Storhaven and be brought over by pony cart and left at the shop in the normal fashion. We just needed to tell Shona that, although the packages would be addressed to me, they could be handed directly to Rose. We had done our business, and were discussing the renovation that would take place next door, when Lyle came in.

"*Morgoni!*" he greeted us. He sounded cheerful enough, but I thought he looked like a man carrying burdens.

"*Morgoni,*" we all responded. Then, "What's up?" asked Malcolm, who is quick to read people.

Lyle dumped his backpack on the floor by the counter. "I've got to head over to Storhaven," he told us. "There's been trouble, and with Stensen gone, there's nobody to sort it out. Verity has asked me to go over… and it seems that the coastguard and the police have left the island without doing anything about the refugees, and Ingrid and Dougie are worried about the press people and this documentary they're making…"

"Surely all that's the business of the *Oyrod*?" asked Shona. "That's why we elect an island council! It shouldn't all fall to you!"

"True," agreed Lyle. "But who do you suppose was chair of the council, elected only two years ago? Fox-Drummin! And who was the secretary? That woman who was also arrested. And most of the *Oyrod* are *harkrav* and blame Verity for everything that's happened, because she's there, in Storhaven, and everyone knows her, and we three are here in Gamla Hus, out of the way!"

"Shall I go over with you?" volunteered Malcolm.

"Not a good plan," pointed out Shona. "Patrick was saying at breakfast that your skills are really needed here, given that you've just renovated your own place."

"I could go over," I suggested. "Would you mind keeping an eye on my chickens, Malcolm? At the very least I could offer Verity moral support."

Lyle looked relieved. "That would be really grand," he said. "I hate to think of Verity trying to deal with all this on her own – and her still being a newcomer to the island."

CHAPTER 4

One of the many joys of living so far north is the speed with which things change. Sunset is five minutes later every day in February, so we feel the spring approaching as the days lengthen, long before the air begins to warm or the plants seem to start growing again. Malcolm had offered us his pony and trap, and I was driving. After several calm days the track up to Fyrtarn Fjell was dry and the ponies took the steep slope with ease. The view from the top was lovely. The island stretched out before us, a thin smattering of bothies and wind turbines, a patchwork of moorland divided by stone walls, a few lonely ruins and a scattering of sheep across the landscape.

Lyle had been quite quiet as we travelled. He was wearing uniform, looking like a proper *nasyoni* or police officer, in honour of the occasion.

"What are your plans?" I wanted to know.

He looked ahead, staring down at the old, ruined chapel and the winding track beyond. "I'll drop you off at Verity's first," he answered. "I need to check in with the people on Shetland, so I'll go to Stensen's office after that – and take stock of the situation. I need to find out the right protocol to deal with a situation where the chair and secretary of the island *Oyrod* are unable to serve…"

★★★

During the time that I had lived on En-Somi, I had been to Storhaven often. The ferry came in there once a week, weather permitting, as in theory it still does, so everything that the island doesn't produce for itself arrives that way. The knitting collective to which I still belong, despite my failing sight, sometimes used to meet at the Old Castle *fi'ilsted* back then, and the council offices are just down the road from the kirk towards the harbour. The BBC Alba documentary called Storhaven a 'sleepy little town' but it never seemed that sleepy to me, and on the day that I am recalling now, it was really quite busy.

In Storhaven there are comparatively few of those tall, imposing constructions you see in some Scottish towns, but Verity lived in a flat in one of them, looking out onto the main street and angled slightly towards the sea. We tied the ponies up by the kirk and walked the few steps back up to Verity's building. Lyle pushed at the door, which wasn't locked, and called up the stairs. "*Hei*, Verity! Are you there?"

Verity came to the landing above and looked down at us, and her face lit up. "*Hei!*" she greeted us. "I'm so glad to see you. Come on up!"

The flat was less tidy than when I was last there. A Bible and several commentaries were lying open on the kitchen table, along with a mug and a plate with a few crumbs, telling the tale of afternoon tea. The washing machine was churning away in a corner and there was a pile of folded clothes on one of the kitchen chairs.

Verity looked around, perhaps seeing the place as we saw it. "I'm having a busy day," she explained, "trying to do too many things at once."

She moved the pile of clothes so that we could both sit down. "I offered to wash the clothes of the refugees," she told us. "Frankie jumped at the chance, but now I see that half their garments are falling apart. I thought the people in the town would be less suspicious of the newcomers if they didn't smell quite so much!"

"They're not really newcomers!" Lyle pointed out.

31

Verity was putting the kettle on and lifting down a biscuit tin which proclaimed the motto, 'All you need is love, but a few biscuits can't hurt!'

"No, they're not newcomers to the island," Verity agreed, "but they're newcomers to Storhaven. Remember, people hardly knew they were out there at the old airport, until a week or so ago.

"And I need to plan my sermon for Sunday. I was hoping to say something people could hold onto, to help them to make sense of all this. I've been thinking about the parable of the sheep and the goats. You know: *'in as much as you do it unto the least of my little ones, you do it unto me'*. But then I think I sound as if I'm justifying my actions in trying to help the refugees. I really want to take everyone's eyes off me…"

"Perhaps you can't," suggested Lyle. "Perhaps folk are bound to look to you, because who else can they look to, just now? Not the *harkrav*, that's for sure!"

We drank our tea and munched on delicious shortcake, before Lyle left on his errands. I helped Verity prepare her spare room and we talked a little about her congregation.

"It isn't all bad news," she told me. "Ingrid and Dougie Fraser and old Holti have organised a communal kitchen for the refugees. It's pretty much stopped the begging. We can go down there, and you can see for yourself in an hour or so. But some people say we're just attracting all the refugees to the town, and that we ought to take the food over to St Matthew's Bay and feed them there, in the old airport… They're sleeping all over the place, the refugees. We let some of them stay in the kirk last night, but that caused a lot of complaints this morning…"

I told Verity about the project we had over on the west of the island, about renovating the ruined bothy. She sighed. "I wish someone over here would suggest such a thing," she commented. "But people are worried. Frightened, even. They feel as if their town has changed – they feel out of control."

"Perhaps Lyle'll sort out what to do about the island council," I suggested. "They could provide the lead we need."

Verity sighed. "Do you know, the *Oyrod* has only met openly once since I arrived. I think they've just been making decisions among themselves, to suit themselves. I talked to Jeannie at the Copper Kettle about it. She didn't even know there *is* an elected island council! And she's been running that tea shop for years!"

"People need someone to take a lead." I was thinking aloud. "If Lyle hadn't invited Si and Rose's family over, and if Shona and Patrick hadn't thought of renovating the bothy next to them, nothing would've happened in Hus either."

"And if there's a problem," Verity agreed, "and there doesn't seem to be a leader, people argue and fall out. That's what's happening here. If only the *Oyrod* would call a public meeting, half the disagreements on this side of the island would go away."

***

The three of us went to the Old Castle *fi'ilsted* for dinner. Lyle had been busy. He had spoken at length to the police on Shetland, and then to someone much higher up in Aberdeen, and was told he was officially Acting Sergeant, at least until the situation became clearer. With the help of Sergeant Stensen's wife, who was still on the island, he had located the official documentation about the *Oyrod* and had discovered that, in the event of both Chair and Secretary being unavailable, the remaining members had to choose others of their number to fill those roles and that the whole council was then obliged to hold a public meeting within one week.

"So, Annie Stensen was willing to help you?" I asked, surprised. After all, Lyle had been responsible for producing recorded evidence proving that the *nasyoni* sergeant was corrupt.

"She's being quite helpful," agreed Lyle. He wrinkled up his nose. "I can't say I like her, though. Everything's about *her* – how her husband has let her down, how she feels people are blaming her for things, how the *harkrav* have always looked down on her… I was with her for an hour this afternoon going through some stuff, and she never once showed any concern for her husband. I got the feeling she was helping me in order to stay in my good books… It didn't work!"

"When I arrived last autumn," Verity told us, dipping a chip into her mayonnaise, "Annie Stensen was one of the women who brought me things for the flat. I got the impression she was quite an important person in the town."

"I think she just fancied herself!" commented Lyle, with unusual meanness. "She's just *bondi*, like the rest of us!"

"I found it really hard to make sense of it all," Verity continued. She looked at me. "It was only when I had lunch with you and Malcolm – do you remember, over in his bothy? – that I really understood the division between the *harkrav* and the *bondii* on the island. And I had no idea how Jeannie fitted in!"

"When Malcolm and I first went to the Copper Kettle," I told the other two, "I got the impression that Jean really hated the other refugees, even though she was a refugee herself at one time. I was amazed that it was she who phoned the coastguard and saved us from those criminals. I thought she was totally on the side of the smugglers."

"She's got a heart of gold," commented Verity. "She's just been used and hurt – really badly hurt. That's all."

"It's when you talk like that," Lyle said, smiling warmly across the table at Verity, "that I can see why you're a minister of a kirk…"

Verity blushed a little. "I'm not so sure…" she said but didn't finish her sentence. Instead, she looked out of the window down towards the dark of the harbour. "They say the weather's changing," she added. "Tomorrow could be a wild day."

★★★

She was right about that.

Lyle phoned Ingrid Fraser the following morning. The wind was howling round Verity's flat, electric wires in the street were humming, clouds were scudding across the sky, coming from the east, from Norway, from the Russian steppes even. He stood in the hallway for better reception, but also to be almost out of earshot, hoping that Verity and I wouldn't hear. We could hear, and we could read the expression on his face too.

He came back into the kitchen where we were still drinking coffee.

"The island council isn't playing ball," he told us.

"What do you mean?" Verity also looked worried.

"They can't agree about who'll take the lead when it comes to choosing a new chair and secretary. Ingrid has tried but Fin Murray says it isn't appropriate for her to make any suggestions, because she wasn't elected to the *Oyrod*. She's the kirk representative. He says it ought to be someone who was elected…"

"Who's Fin Murray?" I asked. I thought I'd heard the names of everyone who lived on En-Somi, but this name didn't ring any bells.

"You met him at the elders' meeting," Verity told me. "Youngish. He was wearing a suit and tie."

"Son of old Fergus Murray," added Lyle. "They used to live over on the south of the island. Fin went off to some posh school in England and didn't come back until old man Murray died. He built that place on Floirean's Cnoc, looking down on the harbour."

"*Harkrav*, then?" I asked.

"Fancies himself as *harkrav* anyhow," agreed Lyle. "But *bondi* two generations ago."

"Well, so will this Fin Murray call a meeting of the *Oyrod*?" I wanted to know. Obviously, someone had to.

"Seems not," said Lyle. "He told Ingrid it wasn't his place…"

Just then the phone rang. Verity sighed and clicked on 'answer'. "Verity speaking," she said, encouragingly.

Immediately we could hear a torrent of words, angrily cascading into the room. We could pick up some of it – the words 'refugees', 'filth', and even *'sommy klinger'*, which is an extremely vulgar corruption of our dialect. The man at the other end was evidently very upset.

Verity stayed calm. When she could get a word in edgeways, she responded with sympathy, saying, "That's awful!" and, "I'm really sorry to hear that," and eventually, "Yes, you're right. Something has to be done."

She sighed when she'd clicked off the phone. "Some of the refugees broke into the ferry office last night. They've left it in a terrible mess. Tom says it's just taken him an hour to clear up. He phoned Sergeant Stensen's number but Annie isn't answering their phone. He rang the number listed for the island council, but it's Fox-Drummin's number, so that wasn't any good either."

"Oh dear!" Lyle looked worried. "If they broke in, I'd better go down there and talk to Tom. But you know what'll have happened? Those who weren't in the kirk've been sleeping in the old stables at the end of Frigg Alley, but the weather turned last night. They probably just needed somewhere warmer and dryer. You can't blame them, in a way."

"I don't blame them," agreed Verity. "But Tom's right, something has to be done. There're fifteen or more homeless people on *En-Somi*! The kirk people are doing what we can – at least, some of us are – but we need a proper solution."

Lyle absent-mindedly poured himself another mug of coffee. "Who are the elected members of the *Oyrod*?" he asked. "Who represents our side of the island?"

We all looked at each other. Then I remembered. "Oh, I think it's the person who owns the land south of Malcolm's place, beyond Jamie's bothy – one of the En-Somi Munros. *Harkrav.*"

"Why did the Gamla Hus people elect a *harkrav* representative?" Verity wanted to know.

"Good question!" responded Lyle, grimly. "There's a long tradition of *harkrav* men standing for election. It tends to work in families, too. I suppose we don't give it as much thought as we should. And I don't know of any *bondii* on our side of the island who'd stand."

"And it's never really been an issue until now," I pointed out.

"Well…" Verity was thinking aloud. "Do we have anyone elected to the council who could call a meeting?"

Once again, we all looked at each other. Then, suddenly, Verity giggled. "Oh! We do!" she exclaimed. "I'm sure we do! Isn't Holti on the *Oyrod*? I remember him saying to me once that the only difference between the island council and an elders' meeting is that an elders' meeting begins with prayer!"

"I'll go round to see him," said Lyle, grinning. "I'd better call on Tom in the ferry office first. Oh, I'd like to see the faces of the *harkrav* if Holti calls a meeting!"

★★★

Verity and I walked down to the kirk with a pile of laundered clothes and four loaves of bread, to find that food was already being served to the refugees. They were sitting in the pews, steaming plates resting on their laps, and here and there I noticed that Bibles or psalm books were being used as improvised lap trays. Frankie, the woman who had seemed to be the leader of the refugees when we first met them, gave me a little wave with her left hand, which was still holding her spoon.

Holti was delighted with our bread offering. "Just what the doctor ordered!" he pronounced and started to tear it into chunks and slather it in butter. "Yon young *nasyoni*, Lyle, seems to be taking a bit of a lead. Did you know, he's got me calling a meeting of the *Oyrod*!"

"I knew he was going to ask you," I chuckled. "Will you do it?"

"Do it? I've done it!" laughed Holti. "Made a few phone calls, pointed out the rules. There was nothing they could do to stop me. Didn't like it, though, I can tell you! Fin Murray, now... I wish you could have heard him! Spluttered like an English prime minister caught out cooking the books!"

"So, when are you meeting?" I wanted to know.

"Tomorrow morning, at 10.00am, then we'll hold a public meeting on Saturday evening, here in the kirk. For everyone. Can you get the Gamla Hus people over here?" He gave me a mischievous grin. "Seems to me it's important the *harkrav* are outnumbered!"

CHAPTER 5

I stayed with Verity for the next couple of days. The ferry arrived, although there was quite a storm and we half expected it to be cancelled. The last of the ordinary journalists left on the boat so that only the BBC Alba people remained. They had embarked with enthusiasm on their documentary – it was to be submitted as part of their degree – and they were delighted that they would be able to sit in on a meeting of the *Oyrod.* They seemed set to stay for a while. Additional clothes had been sent over on the ferry for them, but when I came across them filming the evening food distribution at the kirk, I was delighted to see that the lassie, who I knew by then was called Elise, was wearing a *gensi* which I had knitted. Tom sold the produce of our knitting cooperative down at the ferry port at almost double the price we charged fellow *bondii*. I hoped the young reporters were paid well!

The ferry brought more than the usual number of passengers, especially considering that it had been such a rough crossing. The word had gone out about Saturday evening's open council meeting, and *En-Som-in-Fedii,* islanders who worked on Shetland during the winter, had returned to have their say concerning the refugees. I had been on the phone to Malcolm every day, and Lyle had been back over to Gamla Hus, and together the two men had organised the *bondii* from the west of the island to travel across to Storhaven. The meeting was to be at 6pm. Some of the Gamla Hus people were going to stay the night with friends or family in the small town or in bothies nestled into the surrounding moors.

A few families aimed to head back that night, but they were the minority.

The *Oyrod* had convened in private. They had been unable to avoid meeting, although Holti told us, with a degree of amusement, that some of the *harkrav* found it difficult to believe that he, a mere *bondi*, would have enough initiative to force obedience to the rules.

"They're keeping control of the council, though," Holti told us. "Fin Murray has been chosen as Chair, and Blair Munro as Secretary. They'll try to manage things to suit themselves."

"I'm not sure they can," Lyle remarked. We were sitting in the Copper Kettle, which was buzzing with activity because of some *En-Som-in-Fedii* from Shetland who made up a lively group in one corner. There was a growing number of people from Hus in evidence too. "There're people here I haven't seen for years," he added, and waved to an elderly crofter at the table by the door, who was tucking into one of Jeannie's all-day breakfasts.

"How will it work – this meeting?" Verity wanted to know.

"Everyone who's a resident of the island can attend," Lyle explained. "That includes everyone who works away in the winter but still has an *En-Som-in-Fedi* address for tax purposes. The council should have an agenda, which we'll work through, and everyone can vote on each item. Things are agreed by a simple majority vote, taken by a show of hands. By law, there has to be room at the end for the islanders to raise any additional issues they want to have considered."

Verity was looking round the café. "The kirk will be fuller than I've ever seen it!" She grinned.

★★★

Although the meeting was to be at 6pm, Verity and Lyle left a good hour earlier to arrange the kirk. Extra chairs had been brought in from another room, and lined up next to the three chairs that were normally placed at the centre front, behind the table where communion is served. The council would be facing the rest of the islanders, who would be seated in the pews.

Malcolm and I arrived about thirty minutes later, and more than half the seats had already been taken. The atmosphere didn't seem at all like that of a kirk. From every part of the space came the sounds of people chatting and laughing. There were islanders standing to shake hands or hug each other, climbing across the legs of others to reach the aisles to greet friends or relatives they hadn't seen for a while or turning in their seats to call back to neighbours seated several pews behind them. Ingrid and Dougie Fraser were at the door, distributing photocopied agendas to folk as they arrived, and a small group of children who I didn't know were sitting on the steps at the front, playing jacks with deep concentration. The BBC Alba people had set up their equipment on the small balcony that runs along the back of the kirk.

Dougie offered to find us seats at the front.

"*Nei*, thank you." Malcolm was squeezing into a rear bench beside a couple I assumed were *En-Som-in-Fedii,* and reaching across to shake hands with the woman. "Kirsty and I were at school together in Lerwick," he told me. "In the same class. She lives on Yell now. And you must be Alasdair?"

"I am!" Alasdair was a lanky, blond man with a floppy moustache. "I work on the tidal power generator, but I'm an islander really. I was brought up over beyond Frigg Moor. I'm another of the MacLoughlans. Second cousin to Jamie. *Morimori* Cadha was our great-aunt."

I laughed. So it always is on En-Somi. One way or another, most of the *bondii* are related.

I heard some sort of kerfuffle behind me and turned to see what was happening. "Oh-oh!" I hissed to Malcolm. "This could be interesting!"

Standing in the doorway was Frankie, the woman who seemed to be the leader of the refugees. Behind her I could see others: Charlie and his son Shawn, the young couple Quincy and Mo, and Eric, who had helped to rescue Malcolm and Verity from the waves only a few weeks ago. Frankie was looking determined. Ingrid looked worried. Lyle was approaching from the front of the kirk where he had been talking to a group of well-dressed *harkrav* seated on the left of the aisle.

"We's every right to be 'ere!" Frankie was arguing. "It's our lives what're going to be discussed!"

Ingrid turned to Lyle. "What are the rules?" she asked. Then, to Frankie, "I agree: I think you should be allowed in, but…"

Lyle was turning over the pages of a tattered document, stapled together in one corner. "Well…" Then he grinned. "*Aja!*" he announced. "This is a public meeting. According to the rules anyone may observe, but only *En-Som-in-Fedii* can vote. So, welcome!"

The *Oyrodii,* or island council members, came in, almost like a procession, from the room at the rear, and Ingrid left her place at the back of the kirk and went to join them. An air of formality seemed to have entered the sanctuary with the council members. The children playing jacks returned to their parents, and a hush fell. The refugees were still finding seats. People were shuffling along the pews; children were lifted onto laps to make more space.

I recognised only half, at most, of the council. Holti, of course, I had met, and Ingrid was a friend of Malcolm's; I had been to their Storhaven house a few times. I had seen Fin Murray at the *domstol* – the elders' meeting that Malcolm and I had attended before Solstice – but there were two men I couldn't recall ever seeing before, and a young woman with long, blonde hair who didn't look at all like an islander. I didn't know which of the men was Blair Munro, the official representative of Gamla Hus, until Fin Murray introduced the council.

The agenda was followed scrupulously, and it was, honestly, boring. It seemed to me as if everything that possibly could be, had been listed for discussion: the need for new desks for the school in Storhaven, a request to replace missing cobbles in Frigg Alley, an application for a wind turbine licence for two of the bothies on McGreggor's Moor, a report from the Scottish Fisheries Protection Agency about fish stocks within a five-mile radius of the island, and a request for additional mooring in Storhaven harbour.

"They're stalling on the real issues," Malcolm whispered to me. "Half of this stuff doesn't need a public meeting."

People started to get restless. Over on the right of the kirk a baby was beginning to cry.

"Perhaps the mother of that child would like to take it out?" suggested Fin Murray, looking annoyed. "This is a business meeting!"

There was a murmur of disapproval from the body of the kirk.

"Mothers have as much right to be here as anyone else!" remarked a woman to a small round of applause.

"'Ear 'ear!" called out Frankie.

"Talking of rights…" Fin Murray was getting rather red in the face. "I'm not sure everyone in this kirk even has the right to be here!"

Verity, who was seated near the front, stood. "This is a kirk!" she said. "Everyone and anyone has a right to be here!"

Lyle stood next to her. "And according to the rules," he told us all, while waving in the air the document which was his record of the correct conduct of an *Oyrod* meeting, "nobody may be excluded. Visitors can observe, but they can't vote."

Fin Murray looked angry. Other members of the council turned and spoke to each other. The blonde woman reached forward and tugged at Fin Murray's well-cut jacket. When he turned, she murmured something to him. He turned back to face us all.

"This meeting has so far lasted for an hour and a half," announced Murray. "Your patience has been taxed. We thank you for attending. I have just received the suggestion that we should adjourn and continue our business a week from tonight."

At once several people stood, including Malcolm. "Oh *nei*, you don't!" he called out. "People have come a long way for this meeting! And we haven't started to discuss the thing that concerns us all."

Murray looked slightly flustered, but determined. It occurred to me that he was used to difficult meetings – board meetings, perhaps, or meetings of shareholders. He knew how to manipulate a situation.

Lyle was waiving the rule book in the air again. "Every time the council meets," he shouted, "you're obliged to leave time for concerns of the islanders which were not on the agenda. Look at paragraph 14B. It couldn't be clearer!"

From all around the kirk there were murmurs and grunts of approval. Along the pew from me, Alasdair was chuckling.

"I suggest," said Fin Murray, brazening it out, "that everything we have considered this evening *has* been of concern to our community. I'm not suggesting that we close the meeting, only that we continue it at a more convenient time. There will be an opportunity to raise island matters when the formal agenda has been completed. If you read paragraph 14C, I'm sure you'll find that's what it says."

"'E's trying to pull the wool over yer eyes!" I heard Frankie call out.

A tall woman with red and grey streaked hair rose. "You can't close this meeting without the agreement of the majority!" she pointed out.

Fin Murray looked impatient. "I'm not suggesting we close the meeting," he insisted, "only that we postpone the second half of our business until a more convenient time." He looked around the kirk and added, "There are bairns here who will be longing for their beds!"

Lyle stood again, and turned to face the packed and angry

44

kirk. "Right then!" he called out. "Let's take a vote! All in favour of postponing the second part of the meeting until next Saturday, raise your hands!"

There was absolute silence. The *harkrav* seated along the front row on our side of the kirk looked at each other, and one or two whispered comments to their neighbours. I saw one of them shrug. On the platform, several of the councillors raised their arms. They were entirely alone. Even the *harkrav* on the front row stayed still, just glancing over their shoulders nervously to see what the *bondii* were doing.

Lyle waited a moment.

"It seems to me," he said, "that the will of the islanders is clear. We wish to finish this meeting tonight!"

"Hear, hear!" shouted Alasdair, who was sitting next to me, and his wife giggled.

Fin Murray must have realised that his ploy hadn't worked. "Very well," he said. "So, the next item on the agenda is the extension of the cemetery on Aeloff's Hill. We have received a suggestion that the southern wall be removed and rebuilt along the line of the original boundary, to allow space for between ten and fifteen more graves without encroaching on the moors to the north…"

There was some laughter from around the kirk. We now all knew what the *harkrav* were doing. They would drag the formal business out until midnight if they could, to avoid getting to the subject of the refugees. They were protecting their own vested interests, and we knew it.

★★★

They hadn't reckoned on Holti. I suppose that, until he had called the council meeting, the richer and more influential members had thought that he was just a harmless peasant, representing a small group of *bondii* on a lonely peninsula of En-Somi. In their eyes he had counted for nothing.

45

It was Holti, though, who waited until the business of the cemetery had been agreed, and who then stood and announced, with apparent pleasure, "Any council member can request a comfort break. I suggest we pause the meeting now and reconvene in twenty minutes. I'm told that there's warm punch available at the Castle. Can we take a vote on this?"

A forest of arms was raised in the air. There was laughter and chat, people standing and stretching their limbs, movement towards the door.

"If I were Fin Murray," Malcolm said to me as he handed me my jacket, "I'd be rather worried about the way things are going!" Then, to Alasdair, he asked, "Join Marie and me at the Castle? You'll find it'll not have changed!"

★★★

The punch was good, but judging by the high colour of some of the *bondii* when we returned to the kirk, a reasonable amount of whisky had been consumed too. It was already well past 8pm but there were more people crammed into the pews than before the break. The excited and indignant talk at the Castle had attracted a few Storhaven residents who had been less than interested in the fate of the refugees until now.

I looked across at Frankie and her friends as the seats filled up. "Did you ask Rose and Si to come?" I asked Malcolm.

"I did," he told me. "And so did Lyle, but I think they wanted to stay out of the limelight. And, you know, I think they're tired. Their lives are rather up in the air just now."

"Most of the others are here," I pointed out. "In fact, all of them!"

"Not all." Malcolm was also watching the refugees in front of us. "There's no sign of Jarvis…"

A small, involuntary shiver went down my spine. Jarvis was the only one among the people we had found camped out in the derelict airport to frighten me. Jarvis, with his long dark coat and his blue and white football scarf. Jarvis, who had tried to turn the other refugees against us, who had accused me of stealing from the dead body of little Lavender. Jarvis, whose very presence frightened our little Marigold. *Nei*, Jarvis was nowhere to be seen, and despite my better nature, I was pleased.

It took a while for the meeting to quieten down when Fin Murray called us to order. There were no more items on the agenda, so this was when the real business of the evening would begin.

"Will everyone who has an issue they wish to bring to the council please stand!" instructed Fin.

At once the whole row of *harkrav* in the front pew stood, along with several other people around the kirk.

"Guy Stewart?" called out Fin.

A tall man dressed in a waxed jacket and a cloth cap rose. He was the first in the row of standing *harkrav*. "I would like the council to consider the possibility of paving our roads," he announced, and sat down again.

Murray made a note on his device.

He looked at the next man standing in the front row. "Spencer Fraser?" he asked.

"I want to suggest that we consider introducing the teaching of curling into our island schools," was this man's suggestion.

Another note was made on the tablet.

He called on a woman after that. She wanted the council to authorise the publication of a tourist guide to the island. The next member of the *harkrav* suggested that the island should host an arts and crafts exhibition to coincide with the summer solstice. There were suggestions that we invite our MSP to present end-of-year prizes to the children finishing primary school; that we improve street lighting in Frigg Alley; that signs be put up beside the burn that runs through Storhaven, warning people that it might flood; and even that we petition Holyrood for the right

47

to dual British and Norwegian nationality for all islanders. Each time a suggestion was made, Murray noted it on his device. In no time at all he had a list of a dozen or more 'concerns' which needed to be considered – and so far, none of them related to the refugees.

"What nonsense!" hissed Malcolm under his breath. "They must have planned this during the break."

However, despite the best schemes of the *harkrav*, Murray had to hear from the rest of us sooner or later. To this day I'm convinced that he called on Aileen because she looked so small and timid, a young woman with reddish-blonde hair and pale skin. She had been standing patiently all the while that Murray had been prioritising the *harkrav*, almost like a child in trouble waiting outside a classroom.

"The young woman in the third pew!" called out Murray, pointing to Aileen.

She took a deep breath, still looking down at the head of the person seated in front of her. I felt myself silently urging her: "Go on, Aileen – say something!"

She raised her head, looking directly at Murray, and it seemed to me that her whole body stiffened. "I suggest," she said, calmly and clearly, "that we deal with the most urgent matter facing this island first. What is the *Oyrod* planning to do to help the refugees?"

At first there was a murmur of approval. Then someone in the opposite corner of the kirk started clapping. Others joined in. Malcolm stood. Alasdair stood. Then everyone was standing, clapping, calling out, "Hear, hear!" Some of the younger *bondii* started stamping their feet in approval. I could feel the wooden boards under my feet vibrating.

"Order! Order!" shouted Murray, sounding like something from the televised debates in Westminster.

Slowly, the noise abated. People sat again, many laughing, grinning at their neighbours. People were shaking Aileen's hand.

"We will take the issues in the order in which they were raised!" announced our flustered chairperson.

"Cheat!" called out Frankie. "You asked all them bosses first! I fought what this was a' island council, not a bosses' council!"

"We will do everything in the proper order!" responded Murray, rather pompously.

Then Lyle stood, waving his instruction manual in the air again. "The proper order," he shouted, "is the order chosen by the assembly. Not by the council members. Clause 23A. See for yourselves!"

Another big cheer went up. The council members were looking across at each other anxiously.

When Murray didn't respond at once, Lyle called out again, "All those in favour of dealing with the issue of the refugees next, raise your hands!"

Instantly, hands shot up around the kirk. It was not unanimous. I know from Verity that some of the islanders hoped that the council would quietly get rid of the refugees, as they had no doubt planned, but it was a huge majority. Another cheer went up.

"I've never been in a meeting in a kirk like this before!" exclaimed Alasdair. "It was worth coming over from Shetland just for the last half hour!"

The council members were talking among themselves. There was some nodding of heads, then Murray spoke again.

"We have, of course, been considering the issue of the refugees," he announced. "You seem to have the impression that your council does nothing…"

"*Aja!*" called out someone. "That's just what we think!"

"So, I'll ask Blair Munro to explain our position," Murray continued.

Blair Munro was, I suppose, in his early thirties back then. He wasn't dressed like an islander but like a sportsman, in a blue and white tracksuit, the colours of the Scottish rugby team that year. He wore his hair long and in a high ponytail, aping the style of the island children – or was this a fashion sported by some group to which he belonged on the mainland? He looked entirely at ease. His accent, when he spoke, was pure English, received pronunciation, like something you might have heard on the BBC way back in the 1950s. He looked relaxed and casual, as if the meeting of the *Oyrod* was mere recreation after a busy day spent doing more important things.

"Ladies and gentlemen," he started, then grinned. "Fellow islanders!"

I could hear a few hisses and murmurings coming from the ranks of the *bondii* who crammed the kirk. Here was no fellow islander, whatever his official status.

Munro continued, apparently oblivious to the muttering. "You are concerned – of course you are concerned – about the presence among you of a group of people who you did not invite, who do not know your ways, who have been causing you nothing but trouble, who should have left this island years ago…"

"And why didn't they?" called out someone from one of the pews. "They didn't stay to work with us *bondii*! They were slaves to *harkrav* islanders!"

"*Aja!*" shouted someone else. "Working for members of the *Oyrod!*"

"Shame!" cried someone else, and there was a smattering of applause.

Munro looked unfazed. He smiled slightly and waited for people to settle again.

"Aye, you're right!" he agreed. "It's a matter of great regret to this council that we didn't see what was going on in front of our eyes."

"Not in front of your eyes if you were on the mainland!" remarked a disgruntled voice. I recognised Malchi's accent.

"Not in front of anyone's eyes if they were too scared to leave St Matthew's Bay!" called out Malcolm.

Again, there was a ripple of applause.

Still, Munro looked untroubled. "Well," he continued, "it seems that the *bondii* knew as little as the rest of us, of what was going on. But all that has been resolved now! What we have to do now is to look to the future. Your council has made a decision. We have asked the powers that be to find places for these poor people somewhere more comfortable, where their children can be educated, where there can be gainful employment for the adults…"

"It seems they've been employed all along!" I heard Petter shout out. "And I gather it was quite gainful, but not for them!"

Malcolm stood beside me.

"Aye?" asked Munro, sighing impatiently.

"Are you telling us…" Malcolm sounded indignant. "Are you saying that you've already contacted the Scottish Justice and Communities Directorates, or the Home Office? Before bringing the matter to a public meeting of the *Oyrod*? By what right have you done that?"

For the first time Munro looked, for a moment, unsure of himself.

Then he recovered. He smiled. "Well, we are your lawfully elected representatives!" he pointed out. "We take our responsibilities seriously!"

Malcolm stood again but didn't wait for permission to speak. "You might take your responsibilities seriously," he responded, "but apparently not the law. You are our representatives, not our bosses!"

I heard the rough laughter of Frankie and a couple of the other refugees. Not knowing island dialect, they had called the *harkrav* 'bosses' all along.

Munro turned to speak to the seated council members behind him. When he turned back, that bland smile was on his face again.

"You're right, of course!" he said, smiling in our direction.

"Perhaps I expressed myself badly. No decisions have been made – no decisions could be made without this meeting – we have merely started to explore possibilities."

I could feel the restlessness of the people around me. On the other side of Alasdair, Kirsty was muttering, "Opinionated snob!" People were turning to express their indignation to their neighbours. Munro's public relations smile was bringing frowns to the faces of the islanders – frowns, and some expressions of scorn.

I stood and spoke out, sounding as mild and as non-confrontational as I could. "So, what other possibilities have you started to explore?" I asked.

Munro opened his mouth and then closed it again.

"Good question!" approved Malcolm, seated beside me.

"Well…" Munro swallowed. "Well, we came to the conclusion that there are no other choices," he responded. "All this was discussed ten years ago, when the other refugees left! Most of you were here at the time. You know that this is no place for southerners – English people. They don't belong here!"

"Do you?" called out a woman in a centre pew, and there was more laughter.

Jeannie stood. "I was English," she pointed out, "until I took on island citizenship."

"And she belongs here!" shouted someone else. Again, there was a stamping of feet from some of the younger *En-Som-in-Fedii* scattered around the kirk.

When I look back on it now, I can see that the *harkrav* managed things badly – badly, that is, if they wanted to get rid of the refugees. When we had all entered the kirk ready for the 6pm meeting there had been quite a number of islanders who were worried about these strangers in our midst. The long-drawn-out meeting, the all-too-evident schemes of the *harkrav* and discussions over hot punch in the Castle, had brought those people over to our side. To be honest, I think that by that time in the evening, anything suggested by the *bondii* was going to be accepted with rapturous applause, and anything brought forward by the *harkrav* was bound to be rejected.

Malcolm made good use of the prevailing mood of the meeting. Once again, he stood. "Over in Gamla Hus," he told us all, "we have already agreed to find a home for one of the families. A bothy is being renovated. They want to stay. We want them to stay. I can't believe that the *bondii* on the west of the island are more generous than those of you who live on the east!"

At once Holti, sitting among the members of the *Oyrod*, stood. Almost before Malcolm had had time to seat himself, Holti cried out, "There is room in my home for one or two people. I could do with some younger folk to help with the sheep and the potatoes. I'm not as young as I used to be!"

To my surprise, Tom from the ferry offices stood. "There's a need for someone to help me out," he announced. "There's no money in it, but the assistant's cottage has been standing empty for years. It'd need some work done on it, but there's room for someone there."

Jamie MacLoughlan, from our side of the island, lurched to his feet. "Isn't there a ruined bothy down towards our summer harbour? There's good pasture there. My *pari-pari*" (he meant his grandfather) "used to keep his ponies there all summer, when I was a bairn."

"*Aja!*" Yanni Sinclair was on his feet. "It's on our land, but it'll never be habitable. The sea level's risen, and the storms have got so much worse that the waves smash into the building. We'd do better to rebuild higher up in the moors, west of Norse Hill. We were thinking of building there a couple of years ago, when we thought my brother and his family might come back to En-Somi. We got all the permissions when we were renovating our place. The land over there needs to be worked. And we'd like to have neighbours."

Fin Murray and Blair Munro were exchanging glances. It was obvious that events had taken them by surprise. There was a quick conversation, and Munro sat, turning in his seat to whisper to the blonde lassie. Murray took the lead again.

"Friends!" he called out, and was rewarded with some murmured responses.

"You're no friend of mine!"

"So, we're friends now, are we?"

And from Andy Kullander, loud and clear, "Friends, Romans, countrymen!"

Murray tried again. "Your sentiments do you justice!" he proclaimed, sounding, I thought, both pompous and ridiculous. "But have you thought of the consequences of these kind suggestions? Renovating and rebuilding properties takes time and money. There are children to be considered, who will need to go to school, and schooling costs money. The *Oyrod* will need to make sure that there are tracks to the new bothies; our medical services can barely cope with the existing island population. And we don't know these people. They may be criminals. They're not settled folk like us. They're not even Scottish!"

"Are you?" called out someone from the crowd, and there was another ripple of laughter.

Blair Munro rose again. It was not a good move. There was not a trace of Scots in his voice.

"And there's the question of taxes," he added. "All the things Fin has mentioned take money, and where will the island find that? Are you all prepared to see even more of your hard-earned cash go out in taxation, to support people who don't belong here? When it comes to Solstice, how will you explain to your children that there are no gifts and no fireworks, because the fruits of your labour have gone to help other people's children?"

Fiona Kullander rose. "I'd be proud to tell my bairns that!" she announced.

Andy, her son, sprang to his feet. "And I'd be proud if my

mam told me that!" he shouted, and there was another round of applause.

"You know what the real issue is," Malcolm muttered to me. "The incomes of the *harkrav* are so much higher than ours. They don't want *their* taxes to go up. They're not thinking of the sacrifices *we'd* have to make. They're thinking of their own pockets!"

Along the pew from me, Kirsty had heard what Malcolm said. "*Aja*," she whispered. "That's what this is all about."

Petter and Malchi had been sitting near the front, watching and listening but not saying much until now. At this point, Petter rose.

"Shouldn't the *Oyrod* have started investigating resettlement grants?" he asked. "There *are* resettlement grants for climate refugees, aren't there?"

"There're no more grants available," announced Munro. "Of course we've looked into that. It's the first thing we did!"

From up on the balcony there was a sort of disturbance: movement and then the voice of a lassie calling out, "May I speak?" It was Elise, the girl with the beret from the TV crew.

"Sorry," Munro answered in his posh southern voice. "We only gave you permission to film, not to take part!"

Heads turned to look up at the balcony. I suppose that some people hadn't even known that the television people were up there.

"Let her speak!" someone shouted out.

"Hear, hear!" called out someone else.

Munro sighed. "All right," he conceded. "But make it brief. It's getting late!"

The young woman came forward to the edge of the balcony. "I just wanted to say," she told us, "that you've been misinformed. There *are* still resettlement grants available. My brother works for the Refugee and Displaced Persons people in Fort William. I'm sure he'd help you make the necessary applications."

At that a cheer went up from the *bondii*, and I knew that the decision was made. The islanders are a kind-hearted people, of course. I suppose most folk are, but if the *harkrav* had known us better, it could have been a tougher business, getting the refuges accepted among us. They had assumed that we would be wary of strangers, especially perhaps people from south of the border, and maybe we are a little. But we are fiercely independent and the *harkrav* had made it all too obvious that they didn't care what we thought – that in fact, in their eyes, our opinions didn't count. By their poor management, they had made it into a contest of refugees versus the elite, and we, in Gamla Hus, had already shown that our hearts were with the refugees. The rest of the island followed and felt triumphant in doing so.

The vote was a *fait accompli*. A forest of hands supported the motion that we would try to find homes for everyone who wished to stay here. Holti stood and made a public undertaking that the Oyrod would apply for any grants that were available.

Another cheer went up.

The meeting was formally closed.

As I stood to put on my jacket, amidst the general hubbub of talk and laughter, Frankie turned in the pew where she was still seated, several rows in front of me. She was a tough woman, that one. Back then I knew very little of what she had been through. What I did know was that tears were streaming down her face, unchecked.

CHAPTER 6

Verity looked as if a mountain had been lifted from her shoulders the following morning. Malcolm and I were awake first, and Malcolm was making coffee and toast before Lyle appeared from the box room where he had slept on a camp bed, on and off, for weeks during the last months of that winter. Verity emerged yawning, her hair standing up on end, and grinned happily at us both.

"I haven't slept that well for weeks!" she announced.

"It'll be a weight off your mind," agreed Malcolm. "That meeting last night could have gone either way."

"They managed it badly," I suggested. "The *harkrav*, I mean. They don't understand the *bondii*."

Lyle appeared in the doorway, stretching and scratching his beard. "They live in a bubble of people like themselves," he offered. "Can I smell coffee? Is there any porridge?"

"Not yet," Malcolm answered Lyle, "but there could be. Do you mind me taking over your kitchen, Verity?"

"I love it!" Verity pulled up one of the mismatched chairs to the table. "And yes, porridge for me too. The oats are in the bin on the counter."

Lyle drew up another chair. I started heaping cutlery rather randomly onto the table.

"Of course," Verity added happily, "this is when the real work starts. Finding homes for all those people, renovating bothies, helping the refugees to settle in…"

"And helping the *Oyrod* to keep their word," chuckled Lyle. "Yes, please, Malcolm. That coffee is just what I need. We ought to make a list of all the possible properties…"

"And talk to the refugees themselves," Malcolm reminded us. "We must work *with* them, not *for* them. I learnt that years ago, in Edinburgh."

"*Aja!*" Verity was nodding. "We've got to do a lot of talking…"

"And a lot of listening," agreed Malcolm, doling out thick porridge into four bowls.

"But at least we'll be doing something!" Verity remarked.

Lyle suddenly looked serious. "You know they won't let it go at this?" he asked. "The *harkrav* I mean. They'll hate the fact that their plan to get rid of the refugees was overturned last night. They'll try to make things difficult, and they might even want revenge on the *bondii*. They're used to getting their own way…"

Verity looked calm. She reached over and touched Lyle's hand. "The trouble with the *nasyonii*," she said, "is that your work makes you too suspicious. I don't suppose they're bad people, they just see things differently from us."

Lyle smiled warmly at her, exchanging a look that was so intimate, it was as if Malcolm and I were not in the room. "There you go again!" he said. "Seeing the best in everyone!"

★★★

As far as I can remember we have never had any real committees in Gamla Hus. Nowadays there are groups who take responsibility for this or that at the Quaker Meeting, and there is the knitting collective, of course, but we just meet in the *fi'ilsted* and discuss things. There has never been an agenda or minutes, just general agreement. Over in Storhaven it's different. Back then there was the committee of kirk elders, the island council and some sort of parents' organisation to support the school. It wasn't surprising, then, to hear from Lyle that he and Verity were forming a group to liaise with the Oyrod and the *bondii*, especially those who had suggested property that might be useful.

Back in Hus the focus was on the renovation of the Stewart bothy. The meeting in the kirk had been on a Saturday, and I think it was only a couple of days later, perhaps the following Tuesday, that Robbie Stewart came into the shop while Malcolm was there, and told him that they had just heard: Buck Stewart's bothy was theirs now, and so he and Paula were ready to apply for the necessary licences to install the ground source heat system and the wind turbine. Things were progressing more quickly than we dared hope. Even the torrential rain, the edge of Storm Eliza that was sweeping across the North Atlantic, could not dampen our spirits.

It must have been the same day that Petter spoke to us. Malcolm and I had decided on lunch in the *fi'ilsted*, for no reason other than the fact that Malcolm had wanted to go to the shop to pick up post. We were sitting right in front of the fire when Petter came over to us. He pulled up a little, round stool and sat with us as we tucked into our roast chicken.

"I'm a bit worried about that wee lassie," he said quietly, glancing across to where Marigold was energetically colouring in a picture.

"She's had a rough time," I answered. "She'll settle better when they're in their own home."

"Maybe…" Petter glanced across at the child, who seemed completely engrossed in her drawing. "Did you know that the bairn can't read?"

"Ah!" It was Malcolm, looking across at Marigold and quickly looking away again.

"She's never been taught," Petter continued. "She's over here at the *fi'ilsted* all the time, and she loves to help. Malchi asked her to fetch one of our big catering tins of tomatoes, and she couldn't – the tins don't have pictures on them and she can't read the labels."

"Well, there was no school over at the old airport," Malcolm pointed out.

"But Rose and Si…?" I asked. "Why didn't they teach her?"

Petter looked down at the table, then back at me. "Perhaps we shouldn't assume they're literate," he suggested. "You must have heard about educational standards among the very poor south of the border?"

"You're right," agreed Malcolm. "And not just south of the border. Some of the people I worked with…"

"Shall I talk to Sigrid?" I wondered. "She said we needed more children in the school."

"*Nei!*" Malcolm put his hand over mine. "*Nei*, wait. We need to do this right. First, we talk to Rose and Si, and then we talk to Marigold, and *then* we talk to Sigrid!"

***

Although Si and Rose were spending most of their waking hours at the *fi'ilsted* by then, we actually found them in Lyle's office. Si was bouncing baby Thistle on his knee and singing her some song I didn't know, and Rose was doing something involving knotting string. We stood at the doorway, Malcolm and I, and I saw at once how different they both looked.

Rose glanced up and grinned. "Oh, Marie!" she exclaimed. "Malcolm! Thank you *so* much."

Both of them were wearing new clothes – new to them, at any rate. We had ordered warm winter jackets for the family and a few other items, and some of our order had obviously arrived. I also knew at a glance that other people had given them clothes too. Baby Thistle was wearing a sweet little blue all-in-one garment with seahorses on it. I guessed, because it was blue, that it had come from Robbie Stewart – their youngest was a boy. Si was wearing a cream-coloured cable-knit sweater that I was sure I had seen on Malchi, and Rose was dressed in the pink and blue hoodie I had chosen for her. I had never seen them in anything but shades of brown until now. Somehow their new clothes made them seem younger.

"You're welcome!" said Malcolm. "How's wee Thistle?"

"She's good!" The other difference in Rose was her smile. I think I only realised then how rarely I had seen her without a look of worry on her face. "She slept through the night last night – the first time ever!"

Si paused in his antics with the little one. "I fink it's because Rose's milk is better. We eats more 'ere than we ever did at the old airport."

"And better!" agreed Rose. "I's putting on weight!"

"And Marigold?" asked Malcolm.

"She's okay," Rose answered, but I think she sounded a bit guarded. Then, "She 'asn't made no friends," she added. "Them uver kids don't play with 'er."

It was our way in. "They've all known each other since they were babies," I reminded Rose. "And they all go to school together."

"Marigold could go to school, you know…" suggested Malcolm. "She'd probably soon make friends that way, and it would give her something to do."

That familiar, worried look was on Rose's face again. "Si and me, we weren't no good at school, and Marigold… she can't read 'n' write. The other kids'll all say she's fick, like they did wiv us."

"Would you like Marigold to be able to read and write?" Malcolm asked, almost casually, crouching down and reaching out to Thistle who clasped one of his fingers with her wee hand. "Aren't you a bonny lassie?" he teased.

"I would," answered Si. "But she's our kid. What if she's got our sort of brains, what can't learn?"

Malcolm sat back on his heals, Thistle still grasping his finger. "I dare say you've both got excellent brains," he remarked. "Usually, people don't learn for some other reason, nothing to do with their brains!" He paused for a moment. "I bet we could teach you, and Marigold too!"

"I 'ated school," reflected Rose, picking up her string project again. "I were always in trouble!"

"Well, you wouldn't be in trouble with us!" Malcolm laughed.

★★★

The building work was moving on well, despite the weather. I was impressed by the speed with which the equipment for the ground source heat pump arrived – on the ferry two Fridays later. The wind turbine, we knew from painful experience, would probably take much longer. After that Patrick and Malcolm were able to re-lay the slate flooring and, in his spare time, Petter started to build in furniture in the traditional way. Malchi had offered to pay for the kitchen equipment. I found Rose and Marigold pouring over some brochures in the *fi'ilsted* not long after our conversation about learning to read. Marigold was excitedly pointing out a picture of a range similar to mine. "Look!" she told Rose. "That's a' oven like what Marie 'as got. And this one –" she turned back a couple of pages, "this is like yours, ain't it Malchi?"

"Well spotted!" Malchi congratulated the bairn. "But this one," and he turned another page, "this is the one I'd recommend for you. It's more modern than Marie's and better for baking."

Marigold jumped up and did a little dance. "We's going to 'ave our own kitchen!" she sang. "We's going to bake bread! We's going to cook chicken pie!"

Rose looked at me, her eyes shining with excitement. "I don't know as 'ow I'll ever be able to fank you."

"Thank Malchi!" I retorted. "I've come to arrange some lessons."

"Oh, lessons!" responded Rose. "'Ow 'orrible!" But her eyes were still shining.

★★★

Malcolm insisted that the first session should be like a party, as little like traditional school as possible. He offered a fish-and-chip lunch at his place, and invited Rose's family. He took his ponies and cart up to the village to collect the others, but I had been at his place the night before, so the cold sleet that was driving almost diagonally across the island didn't bother me. "We can't let them carry that wee baby all this way!" explained Malcolm as he sorted out his ponies. "Today has got to be fun from beginning to end!"

Neither of us had ever formally taught children, but we had both raised them, and so we weren't daunted by the thought of teaching Marigold. I was, anyhow, convinced that she was a very bright little body. She asked questions and remembered the answers, she wanted to know how everything worked, she was even learning some of the island dialect. Her parents still referred to 'the bosses', but Marigold called them *harkrav*, and she spoke of the *fi'ilsted* not 'the pub'. It sounded a little strange, these local words mingled with her very English way of speaking, and rather sweet.

We started right at the beginning. Both Rose and Si knew the alphabet and recognised upper- and lower-case letters, but Si couldn't put them in order. Marigold recognised the letter M as a capital, because it was the beginning of her name, "And I knows that one," she boasted, pointing to a capital L. "because it's for Lavender."

"Perhaps your mam can show you which letter is for Thistle?" suggested Malcolm, and with only the slightest hesitation, Rose pointed to the T. Marigold looked at her mother, impressed. "You can already do it!" she exclaimed, and Rose laughed.

"No, I can't!" she answered. "Never could!"

And so, we were on our way. At first, the fact that Rose and Si knew all their letters, and some easy words, meant that they were ahead of their daughter, and Marigold was full of admiration. She caught up very quickly, though, and within a couple of weeks, she had overtaken them. After that we taught them separately. Malcolm requisitioned one corner of the *fi'ilsted* for the adults' lessons, but Marigold liked to come to my bothy, and as well as reading and writing, I started to teach her ordinary domestic skills. We made cakes and pies, and baked bread, and I answered endless questions. She would arrive sometime in the morning, wearing the bright red jacket that Malcolm and I had bought her, looking for all the world like one of the local bairns, and from the moment she opened my door until the time she left, I would be answering questions and explaining things. I couldn't remember Duncan ever being so demanding, but I loved it.

It was during one of those visits that Marigold asked me, apparently out of the blue, "Does you fink Verity will marry Lyle?"

I had noticed before that one of the many issues that captured the child's imagination was to do with relationships between adults. She had been ahead of me in realising where things were going between Malcolm and me, and very approving when matters developed as the bairn thought they should. We were reading AA Milne poems when she asked me, and I could see no connection between the King's Breakfast and Lyle's marital status, but the child had been right before.

"I don't know," I replied. "Do you think she will?"

"*Aja*," said Marigold, answering with our local word, for the first time as far as I could remember. "I does. I 'opes what I can be a bridesmaid. My mum was a bridesmaid once an' she 'ad a dress to wear like a princess!"

"Well then," I suggested, "we'd better keep our fingers crossed!"

★★★

Over in Storhaven things were progressing too. The *Oyrodii*, forced by the interest of the BBC Alba crew and the group headed up by Verity and Lyle, were in contact with various officials on the mainland. The first result of this was that we were asked to compile a list of all the refugees left on the island – first names and last names and national insurance numbers. This demand actually led to almost insurmountable problems. The refugees, of course, had no idea what official numbers were listed against their names. I dare say even before whatever climate catastrophe had turned them into refugees, most of them couldn't have given anyone that information. In fact, I don't suppose many of the islanders could either, without rooting out some ancient official document!

Lyle and Verity came over to Hus one Monday. I know it was a Monday because my son Duncan and I Skyped at weekends, and I was excited – his term finished towards the end of March, and he hoped to be back on En-Somi, weather and ferries permitting. He was in school in Lerwick, boarding as most of our older children did in those days, and he had been to his father's in Norway for Christmas. I hadn't seen him since October, before I met Malcolm, before I knew about the refugees, but we had talked every week that the weather and internet allowed.

"So why do you have to draw up these lists?" Malcolm asked.

He and I were in the village shop picking up our post. Patrick was dusting some shelves and Shona had made us tea. She brought out more mugs for Verity and Lyle when they came in.

Verity laughed. She was looking happy and ridiculously young to be the minister of the island's only kirk.

"Well, really, of course the work should fall to the *Oyrod*," she told us, with that grin that had become so familiar. "But Blair Munro suggested it might be easier if we did it. The refugees know us better and trust us."

"And I don't want the *harkrav* scaring off these people," Lyle added. "They would dearly love to get rid of the lot of them!"

"What, still?" Shona was handing out shortcake. I'm surprised they ever made a profit with that shop, treating it, as they sometimes did, like a free café!

"It's all to do with the island taxes," Malcolm suggested,

65

sipping his tea. "It'll be because of our separate system, separate from most of the other islands. Well, you know that. Our taxes are lower than the usual Scottish arrangement, lower even than in England, because we're semi-independent. The *harkrav* love that. If they register all their assets here, they save a lot of money."

"But on the downside," I considered, "the island is responsible for more of the services provided for us *En-Som-in-Fedii*. So now, with all these refugees needing help and assistance, they're thinking about their pockets."

Patrick came down the ladder that had enabled him to reach the highest shelves. "Four large tins of baked beans," he told Shona. "Only a month to go before their sell-by date. Lyle, can you take them over to Storhaven when you go back? Holti will be able to use them for his free kitchen."

"Is that still going?" I was surprised.

"It is," Lyle told me. "The *Oyrod* has claimed some sort of temporary support grant but somehow the money doesn't go directly to the refugees. I don't understand why. So Holti's still feeding them in the kirk."

Patrick picked up his mug. "When I was a wee bairn," he told us all, "this island was a sort of tax haven. Then the Scottish and English governments were forced to clamp down – it was after all that fuss about multi-nationals not paying taxes in the countries where they did business." He took two great gulps of tea. How was he able to swallow it when it was still so hot? "It was us, Jersey, the Cayman Islands and Bermuda, I think."

"*Aja.*" Malcolm was crunching his shortbread. "And somewhere else – somewhere obscure… I know! The British Virgin Islands!"

"So how many refugees have you got on your list?" I wanted to know.

"Over in Storhaven, fourteen," Verity told us. "Six of them are under sixteen. It's not exactly an invasion! When you think of the numbers of refugees that used to arrive on some of those little Greek islands and during the invasion of Ukraine…"

"So, with our four, it's still less than twenty newcomers!" pointed out Malcolm.

"You're looking at it from a *bondi* perspective," laughed Lyle. "It's eight children who have to be educated, several couples who might have more children, nineteen people who might need medical attention and who, one day, God willing, will grow old. Nineteen people that the *harkrav* really don't want to support! It all adds up! Come on, let's go and see how much Si and Rose can tell us. I bet they don't even know that they have national insurance numbers!"

CHAPTER 7

You might remember the March of that year. The international news was all about the big fires in Siberia and all across Northern Europe and about the last vestiges of the glacier in Glacier National Park in the US melting away. The pollution from the smoke gave us beautiful sunrises and sunsets when we weren't experiencing storms. Eliza was followed by Fabio, Gabrielle and Hamza in such quick succession that there were arguments about whether we were experiencing four weather events or two. It was the year that the Palace of Westminster in London flooded for the first time. The waves in the summer harbour came crashing in with such force that the ruined bothy belonging to Yanni Sinclair was finally and completely destroyed, proving his point that if we wanted to house any refugees over there, we would have to rebuild much higher up on the moor.

Meanwhile, all these events were overshadowed, for me, by what was going on locally. Verity had persuaded the members of the *Oyrod* to part with some of the grant money from the Scottish government, to buy soft furnishings for the almost-renovated bothy next to the shop. I don't think the way Patrick connected the second bothy's power source to his turbine was strictly legal, but it made it possible to have light and heat in the property until such time as they had their own turbine. The BBC Alba people were filming the renovation – they seemed to be filming everything.

And Duncan came home for the Easter holidays.

I had been very worried that he wouldn't make it. The ferry from Lerwick was timetabled to call in every Friday in those days, just as it is now, but the North Atlantic had proved to be too wild for even that intrepid little boat, and during that whole month it arrived in Storhaven only once. It was our good fortune that the ocean calmed down just long enough for the children from Shetland to make it home.

Malcolm drove me over with his pony and trap. It was a wildly windy day. Towards the top of the Fyrtarn Fjell pass, where the track is most exposed, I wondered whether we would be able to make it, but the ponies were sturdy little beasts and Malcolm was calm and soothing with them, and the going was easier once we had the hill behind us.

Even on En-Somi we could see the signs of those giant storms. There were no trees on the island then, of course, but exposed stone walls had been toppled and there was water standing on the marshier patches of moorland. Sheep were huddled on the sheltered sides of rocks and grassy mounds, and black-backed gulls were wheeling and screaming in the air above us. I remember that I was ridiculously excited.

We tied the ponies up at the kirk, and Malcolm went off to have a cup of tea with Holti, and to talk about the feeding program. We hoped that the duvets, pillows and other bed linen for the new bothy would be in the ferry cargo, but we weren't sure. The storms had played havoc with transport right across the northern hemisphere, and supply chains, already made unreliable by the crazy weather, had collapsed altogether in some regions.

I walked down to the ferry port. Tom was out and about, wearing his high-vis jacket and greeting everyone by name. He was always rather a favourite of mine – when I had first started knitting as part of the cooperative, it had been Tom who had suggested I should sell some of my wares at the port. He had worked down at the harbour all his adult life, so he had seen generations of children catching ferries to Shetland for school and coming home for their holidays taller and noisier. He had known Bjorn from those days and was kind to me, an outsider, settling on the island.

The arrival of the ferry at the beginning of the school holidays was something of an event, and already there were clusters of Storhaven parents standing in sheltered places, talking about this or that. The BBC Alba crew was filming, of course. Quite a lot of the conversation was in dialect, which they seemed to find fascinating.

Even in the harbour, the sea seemed rough, and every now and then a sheet of spray rose in the air as the waves smacked against the rocks that sheltered Storhaven from the worst of the weather. The ferry, when it appeared, looked so small against the grey, heaving backdrop of the ocean, its red funnel standing out in the bleak scene, seeming to nod back and forth as the little ship navigated the waves. The buzz of conversation grew louder, and phones pinged as passengers made contact with those waiting to meet them. Tom was stretching a chain from one hook to another to mark the edge of the quay and to stop people falling in, although I have never heard of such an accident happening.

Then the ferry was turning, backing into her allotted place. The gangplank was lowered and the passengers started to descend, windswept and happy to be home.

I saw Duncan at once. His dark hair was shorter and lighter than it had been in the autumn, and he seemed to have grown about ten inches, but there he was, my son, laughing and talking to his friend Alana, then seeing me, saying something to the lassie, and running down the gangplank, throwing himself into my arms, almost knocking me over.

"Mam!" he said, and that was all, before he gave me another big hug.

Alana stood a foot or two behind Duncan. She is the youngest of Patrick and Shona's brood, and the two had been friends since Duncan was a toddler.

"*Hei*, Marie!" she seemed a little shy. "Mam said you'd give me a lift…?"

Duncan looked over his shoulder and grinned at her. I turned to the girl and hugged her too. "Welcome home, both of you! We're hoping some stuff we've ordered will be on board. Malcolm's coming down to check soon. Would you like to visit the Copper Kettle, to fortify yourselves for a windy ride home?"

★★★

Duncan knew about Malcolm, of course, but they had never met. Malcolm came up to the café and found us eating doughnuts and drinking hot chocolate. There were a couple of other teenagers with parents there too, although those who lived relatively close to the harbour must have gone straight home.

"*Hei*, Duncan! *Hei*, Alana!" Jean was cheerful, doing good business and enjoying it. "Back for the holidays? Goodness knows if you'll ever get away again! *Hei*, Marie!"

When she had left our table, Duncan said quietly to me, "She's in a good mood! I've never seen Jeannie look so happy!"

"It's ever since the refugees were freed," I told the kids. "She always seemed like a bit of a loner – friendly enough, but not really *bondi* or *harkrav*. Rumour had it that Fox-Drummin had invested in the café and I suppose she felt she owed him something. And actually, when we – Malcolm, Verity, Lyle and I – were watching the refugees, trying to see what was going on, it seemed to us as if she was working with them. But then we found out that it was she who called the coastguard and the police. We wouldn't have been able to bring down those scoundrels if she hadn't done that. Now we all know she's one of us." I looked across to where Jean was taking an order, laughing at something a teenage customer

71

had said. "The whole island knows. I think she feels she really belongs, at last."

Perhaps I should have been worried about Duncan meeting Malcolm, but as far as I can remember, I never considered that they might not get on. And I was right. Malcolm bustled into the Copper Kettle, his hair and beard looking tousled, his jacket open showing the *gensi* I had knitted him underneath, and a generally ramshackle air about him, and Duncan stood up at once, even before Malcolm reached our table, and held out his hand.

"You must be Malcolm!" he said. "*Hei!* You look just like Mam described you! And you're wearing something she knitted!"

Malcolm took his hand, and they shook, like a couple of adults. "*Hei!*" answered Malcolm. "I've heard so much about you – all good!" Then, turning to Alana, he said, "And I can see you're Shona's daughter. Did you have a good crossing?"

Everyone sat again. "It was a bit rough," Duncan admitted. "We were okay, but some people were sick."

"And they made us wear life jackets if we wanted to go up on deck," added Alana, wrinkling up her nose.

"Which we did!" agreed Duncan. "Who wants to sit and look out of steamed-up windows on a day like today?"

We dropped Alana off at the shop, and Malcolm took us part way down the track to my bothy. There's a sort of turning point, and after that the going isn't very good for ponies and a cart. We climbed down there and walked the final stretch, arriving home late afternoon. Already, by the end of March, sunset is around 8pm, but the sun seems to hover low in the sky for hours before that. It came out from behind the clouds, briefly, just as we turned the bend and could see the bothy. Behind it the sea was sparkling: there were *muckle scarfs* swooping and wheeling round the stacks and the wind was blowing directly into our faces.

"Oh, it's wonderful!" breathed Duncan. "Better than Norway!" Then, typical of a growing boy, "What's for dinner?"

★★★

The meeting between Duncan and Marigold was less predictable. The child had become very attached to me, perhaps a little possessive, and Duncan was the only child of a single parent, used to having my undivided attention. Of course, they knew about each other, but they had never met.

That happened the morning after Duncan got home. He had slept in, a new development for me. He had always been an early riser, but he was growing up. I reminded myself that teenagers often lie in bed late into the morning. I remember that he was sitting in the rocking chair that used to be his pap's, many years ago, eating a bowl of porridge and telling me about his teacher of Norwegian. "She's from Syria," he was saying. "Or her mam and paps were. She was born in Norway. She still wants to go back, sometime, if she can, but I don't think she will. She's getting married in the summer and then there'll be kids... she's a really good teacher. She's been teaching us how to ask someone out on a date..."

Just at that moment the door opened, and there was Marigold. "'Ello," she said, not coming in, just standing there.

Duncan looked at me and raised an eyebrow. Then he said, mimicking the voice I used to use when he was little and I was telling him the story of the three bears, "Who's been sleeping in my bed?"

We realised afterwards that Marigold didn't know the story. I suppose she just saw a tall, lanky boy, an older boy, a boy who actually belonged there, and heard a strange, angry voice making an accusation which she couldn't deny. She looked at me and then burst into tears and backed away, closing the door, leaving herself standing outside.

"Oh, *nei!*" Duncan jumped to his feet, spilling milk on the floor, running to the door in his bare feet. He swung it open in a hurry so that it banged against the clothes hooks, and rushed outside.

I almost followed him. Then, just in time, it occurred to me that this was something I needed to let them sort out. I finished making a pot of tea and listened.

"Marigold!" Duncan sounded remorseful. "You *are* Marigold, aren't you? Did I scare you? I didn't mean to. I was just fooling around."

Marigold said something under her breath, something I couldn't hear.

Then came Duncan's voice again. "*Nei!* I've been looking forward to meeting you. Mam loves having you here."

Again, a muffled and inaudible response from the child.

"*Aja!* She told me so herself. She told me she's teaching you to read. And she says you're really bright. And that we might make hot cross buns together for Easter, you, me and Mam, because you've got all the makings of a good cook! Unlike me!"

This time I could hear Marigold. "Did she really say that?" and then, "What's 'ot cross buns?"

Duncan laughed. "Special breakfast buns for Easter. But you'll never find out if you stay out here!"

They came in, Duncan leading Marigold by the hand. She was still looking a little wary, but there were no more tears.

Duncan picked up his porridge bowl again. "I'm still having breakfast," he announced. "Have you had any? I'm sure Mam'll make you some."

Marigold sat on the settle, a safe distance from my son. "I 'as my breakfast at the *fi'ilsted*," she said. Then, slightly reprovingly, "In the morning, not in the middle of the day!"

Duncan laughed. "Oh, good one!" he exclaimed. "So, stay to lunch with us! She can, can't she, Mam?"

★★★

An unlikely friendship developed. Well, perhaps it was not as surprising as it seemed to me then. By the time we had eaten lunch Duncan and Marigold seemed to be on really good terms. She went over to the shelf and brought down my photo of Duncan in his school uniform, ready to go off to secondary school. She held it next to him, looking at the likeness.

"You's not as good-looking in real life as you is in this picture!" she announced.

Duncan took it in good part. "*Nei*," he agreed, "but I'm taller."

"'Ight ain't everything!" remarked Marigold.

"*Nei*," Duncan agreed. "It's brains that matter, and Mam says you've got loads of them. Can you read me something?"

Marigold had graduated to the *Just So* stories by then. When she had read all of *How the Leopard Got His Spots*, with very little help from my son, I suggested we go down to the beach.

"After all these storms," I told Marigold, "there could be lots of driftwood."

"Yeah! Yeah! *Aja!*" Marigold was enthusiastic. "I loved collecting stuff off the beach when… before."

"We'll need the sledge," Duncan reminded me. "There could be loads."

"Oh!" I had just remembered. "I think Andy Kullander still has it. He and Christian were collecting wood for Solstice."

"Well…" Duncan didn't look at all daunted. "I wanted to catch up with Andy anyhow! Marigold, shall we go to the Kullanders?"

"What's that?" the bairn wanted to know.

"Not what – who!" explained Duncan. "Do you mean you've never been to the Kullanders? The big red house up on the hill? We need to go there – now! Mam, is that all right?"

They must have picked up Alana on the way through the village. The next thing I knew was that the four of them had planned a major scavenging trip for the following day: Duncan, Marigold, Alana and Andy. Marigold was, of course, by far the youngest, but maybe that wasn't such a bad thing. And they were good bairns. They would look after her.

CHAPTER 8

Olaf told me once that in the middle of the twentieth century, after the two world wars, there was no real ship building on En-Somi. There had been, but the skills had died out. This was not surprising – there is no native woodland. The islanders bought their small, four-man rowing boats, part constructed, from Norway. World War 2, however, had made the *En-Som-in-Fedii* aware of how precarious it was to depend on one other nation for something so essential. During the occupation of Norway, it was impossible to trade with them, and people started to think about other ways of building our own boats. It was the two Munro brothers (Elijah and Noah) who started importing raw wood from Scandinavia, Scotland and even further afield, and that was when our present carpentry skills really developed. By the time I arrived on the island, the tradition was well established of building or mending boats in the winter, and fishing from the middle of spring until the storms made it too dangerous in the autumn. Unlike the people of other islands, we have never fished seriously in the winter or gone out in larger boats a long way from shore. We were then, and still are, largely subsistence fishers, although we do export some mackerel products to niche markets in Edinburgh and London.

As I got to know the people of Hus, when I was a new arrival, it seemed to me as if every man on the island, and quite a few women, had their own carpentry tools, but of course it is like everything: some people were much more skilled than others. Petter, for example, and my Bjorn, were both able to do almost anything they wanted with wood, whereas Alf Kullander couldn't knock a wooden pole into the ground without breaking it, according to his wife. I was not at all surprised, when Malcolm and I visited the new bothy, to see Petter, Yanni and Si standing in the middle of the main room, looking up at the newly constructed bunk bedding and discussing, with great animation, the need for proper steps to the higher level.

"Wow!" I exclaimed, looking around. The place had changed beyond recognition. It looked smaller than when I had last seen it because the bunks, six feet wide, allowing two people to sleep on each level, took up a lot of space, and the kitchen was all installed in the south-western corner. Traditionally, of course, there were no washing machines or fridges in bothies, so that area of the room was more extensive than it would have been in the old days. Old Buck Stewart had made do with a sort of stone and corrugated iron lean-to as a bathroom, but Shona had insisted that the men construct a proper stone bathroom in its place.

"*Hei*, Marie! *Hei*, Malcolm!" we were greeted. Then, "Would you put sliding doors on these bunks, like the ones Bjorn built for Duncan's bed? Doesn't it get stuffy in there, if you close them?"

I laughed. "I only ever use those doors to hide an unmade bed or laundry piled up, waiting to be sorted!" I told them. "But I would add the doors, all the same. At least they'd be there if they wanted them." I grinned at Si. "Rose might want to use them the way I do."

Malcolm was looking around the neat little room. "Is there enough storage here?" he wanted to know. "A family of four can accumulate a lot, even living simply."

I was surprised by Si's response. "That's okay, Malcolm," he told us. "Rose is making 'ammocks."

"Hammocks?" I asked.

"We 'ad them in one of the camps," Si told us. "There weren't no cupboards, so we rigged up 'ammocks using sheets, and 'ung 'em from the ceiling. Lyle 'ad these big balls of string, and Rose is making 'ammocks to go there," he pointed to an area by the small, east-facing window, "and there." He pointed to the area by the door through to the bathroom. "Kitchen stuff'll go in them cupboards Petter made."

"Wow!" I said again. "So, everything's nearly ready?"

"The duvets and the pillows came on the ferry," Malcolm said, "but no bed linen and no chairs."

Si was looking round the room, a strange expression on his face. "That bloke Alf, with the funny last name, 'e said 'e'd lend us sheets and that, and we ain't sat on no chairs for years, until we came over 'ere to Lyle's 'ouse. We'd like to move in as soon as possible if that's okay? Get out of Lyle's way."

"We ought to build these steps up to the top bunk, first," suggested Petter.

"We could do it in a day," pointed out Yanni. "Especially if we had a wee glass of something to encourage us!"

"So, Saturday?" I wondered. "Si, would that suit you? Before the kids go back to Shetland."

"The day before Easter," Malcolm added. "I'll cook those lamb chops I promised Marigold. But check with Rose, Si – we don't want to rush her."

★★★

As I came out of the bothy, leaving the four men to debate the steps that needed to be built and the exact construction of the doors to the sleeping area, I saw Duncan, Marigold, Andy and Alana. They were pulling our old sledge and laughing about something. Marigold rushed up to me.

"We's going scavenging!" she announced. "Petter and Malchi said as they could use the wood…"

"We're off down to our beach, if that's all right, Mam?" I had the feeling that they would have gone there anyway.

"*Aja*," I agreed. "I've just been looking at your new home, Marigold. What do you think of it?"

"'S nice," the bairn answered, looking down at her feet. "I's going to sleep on the bottom bunk, and when she's big enough Thistle's going to sleep next to me. And we got a' oven and a washing machine, but Mum says she's forgotten 'ow they work. And we'll 'ave a' 'dress. What's a' 'dress, Marie?"

Duncan laughed. "Oh, you're wonderful!" he exclaimed. "You'll have an *address* – it's the place in all the world where you live, and people can send you letters."

"What letters?" Marigold wanted to know. "'O would send us letters? Why?"

"Well, you know…" Andy looked sightly perplexed. "When people want to tell you things. Like, the school in Lerwick, when they told Mam and Paps I could defer for another year. Or when Uncle Alec sent out invitations to his wedding in Australia!"

"But the bothy needs a name," Alana pointed out.

"Why?" Marigold wandered.

"So that people know where you live. Like our house is called 'The Shop' and Lyle's house is called *Nasyonihuss*. What's your house called, Marie?"

"*Bjornhuss*," I told them. "It really belongs to Bjorn."

"You could just call it – oh, I don't know your surname!" Duncan sounded quite surprised. Then, seeing the confusion on the bairn's face, he explained, "Your last name. Your family name."

"We ain't got no family name!" asserted Marigold, with great confidence. "We ain't no islanders!"

"Everyone's got a family name!" Andy started to expostulate, but Duncan cut him off.

"It doesn't have to be a family name," he said. "It could be anything. Like – oh, I don't know. Perhaps 'Sea view'?" he suggested.

"We can't see no sea 'ere," pointed out Marigold. "Just Fyrtarn Fjell and moors and tracks and sheep…"

Alana giggled. "'Sheep View' doesn't sound quite right," she told the others.

"We could call it 'Si and Rose's 'ouse'," suggested Marigold.

"Not really 'house'," pointed out Duncan. "That makes it sound like somewhere in a town. What about 'Si and Rose's cottage'?"

"Too much of a mouthful," was Andy's verdict. "Just 'Rose Cottage' would be better. Would your paps mind being left out?"

"'E wouldn't mind," Marigold was sure. "'E loves my mum. But it don't sound like what it belongs 'ere."

"You're right," Duncan agreed. "It sounds like somewhere south of the border, in Surrey or Hampshire…"

"What about using dialect?" Andy suggested. "Doesn't 'Rose Cottage' translate into '*Bothan Ros*'?"

"You're the dialect expert!" Alana pointed out. "But it's a good name. It sounds right. Come on, let's go down to Duncan's beach!"

As they left, I saw Marigold fall into step beside my son. The last thing I heard before they were out of earshot, was, "Duncan, what's a Surrey or a 'Ampshire?"

★★★

We had a little party to welcome them into their new home. Shona had rigged up her Christmas fairy lights around their door, and, true to his word, Malcolm was cooking lamb chops. Rose ensconced herself in her kitchen and made tea, a skill she had re-learnt while they were living at Lyle's, and Marigold, Duncan and I provided the hot cross buns that we had made, with much hilarity, that morning. It was an odd feast but somehow appropriate. Lyle and Verity dropped in for a little while, and all the men who had worked on the building made an appearance. Si looked proud, holding a gurgling Thistle on his hip and greeting everyone with a slightly self-conscious "*Hei!*" Malchi provided a huge plate of sausage rolls, but the *fi'ilsted* was open and quite busy, so they weren't able to be there themselves.

Malcolm had carved a sign on a piece of driftwood: '*Bothan Ros*', and then in smaller letters, 'Home of Rose, Si and family'. We made a little celebration of hanging it next to their door, and Lyle insisted on pouring whisky on it. "Like launching a boat!" he explained.

And then we all went home, leaving the first of our refugee families to settle in.

CHAPTER 9

I had become quite used to seeing the BBC Alba crew around, but I think that until the time I am recalling now, I had hardly spoken to them. They were still based at our friends' home in Storhaven, although they came over to Hus more often than most folk from the east of the island. They liked the *fi'ilsted* and they were fascinated by Olaf, the songs he composed and sang and the history and legends they contained. They had visited the school and interviewed some of the children about their lives on the island, and they had some very dramatic shots of huge waves rolling up into the summer harbour and crashing against the rocks that used to protect our ancestors from the worst that the winter storms could throw at us, before sea levels had risen and the hurricanes had worsened.

I was walking up to see Sigrid that morning. It must have been only a few days after the house-warming at Bothan Ros, because Duncan was still on the island. Alana, Andy and Marigold had called for him before I left home. They had hoped to take Marigold up to the top of Fyrtarn Fjell but the weather was too bad, so instead they were going to walk down to the summer harbour to look at the waves and then to build a fire somewhere over on Hunger Moor and cook hot dogs. The idea, it seemed, was Patrick's. He used to do the same thing when he was a lad. Personally, I wondered whether they would manage to light a fire and keep it burning on such a day, but they would only find out by trying.

Anyhow, Sigrid and I wanted to talk about the knitting cooperative. It was Sigrid's idea. She thought that we might put on lessons for the refugee women, teaching them to knit (if they didn't know already) and then they could join us, and we might expand the reach of our business. Tom made steady sales down at the ferry terminal, to sailors from other islands or the mainland looking for gifts for family. Sigrid wondered, if we could increase our production, whether we might persuade someone on Shetland to carry a stock of our *gensii*. She had ideas about socks and gilets too.

It was a wild day – perhaps I should say, *another* wild day. We can't see the sea from the village, we're protected by hills and moorland, but we could hear it and I could taste the salt in the air. Overhead, dark clouds were heaving and rolling across the low sky, and there was cold rain in the wind.

Just as I arrived at the crossroads by the shop, a pony-driven cart arrived, down from the Fyrtarn Fjell pass. The BBC Alba people and all their equipment were huddled in the back, their hoods up, looking cold.

"*Hei!*" I greeted them. "I bet it was windy up on the top!"

The girl, Elise, pulled off her hood and grinned at me. "It was!" she agreed. "I've never known weather like this!"

The cart pulled up next to the shop. The driver, a Storhaven man I hardly knew, and the two men from the BBC all went inside. Elise came over to me.

"You were one of the people who tracked down the villains, weren't you?" she checked. "Ingrid told us. You're friends with them, aren't you – with Ingrid and Dougie?"

"*Aja,*" I agreed, "but I can't talk to you about that – they haven't been brought to trial yet. The *nasyonii* – the police – warned us not to give interviews."

"But you can talk to us about other stuff?" the lassie insisted. "Your life here and your views about other things… we came here only to report the story as the news broke, originally. You know, refugees held as slaves, illegal arms manufacturing and sales. But now we're making a full-length documentary. Most people in Britain don't know much about En-Somi, and we think it might do particularly well in the States too. Only we'll have to use subtitles because some of it will be in dialect, and anyhow, Americans would never understand your accents!"

I laughed. "*Aja*," I agreed. "I can talk to you about anything else!" Just then a particularly strong gust of wind nearly knocked us both over. "But not out here!" I suggested.

***

Sigrid and I had planned to meet in the *fi'ilsted*, of course. Like Duncan and the other bairns, Sigrid was on school holiday. She had spent the Easter weekend over at her daughter's in a bothy outside Storhaven, helping to look after her newest grandchild, but she was back now, dividing her time between preparation for the new term and the co-operative. We agreed that the Alba crew could join us, as long as they only recorded things we agreed to. Neither Sigrid nor I wanted any record of us talking about knitting lessons or anything else to do with the refugees. Their story, we felt, was for them to tell – them, and them alone.

Petter served us coffee, and the Alba crew and the driver of their cart left their equipment with their jackets by the door. We settled in a semi-circle around the grate where a fire had just been lit. Other than us, the place was empty.

Sigrid had obviously already had dealings with the young *un-fedii* before.

"How's it going, Elise? Jacob? Ollie?" she wanted to know. "Have you all made contact with your families? Were you able to put their minds at rest?"

"Aye!" It was the young man, Ollie, who answered. He was wiping his steamed-up glasses on a handkerchief, looking absurdly young and undressed without them. "My parents weren't too worried – Dad worked for the BBC once; he knows they look after their own. It was your parents, wasn't it, Elise?

Knowing their daughter was out here on an island they had never heard of, and all these hurricanes sweeping across the Atlantic!"

Elise grinned. She was, I realised, a beautiful girl. I had only seen her with a beret on before – she seemed to wear it a lot of the time, but now, with her head bare, I could see the meticulous arrangement of her hair, in tight cornrows with some sort of red, shiny twine braided in with them. She had a high forehead and huge, dark eyes. Once again, she was wearing the *gensi* which I had knitted – the Fyrtarn Fjell winter design, in greens and blues against a natural wool background. It set off her dark skin wonderfully.

"I'm the first of the family to work in the media," she told me. "Dad's a doctor and Mum's a counsellor. I'm sure they think I've left civilisation altogether. I keep telling them, I haven't even gone abroad! This is still part of Scotland. But they remember stories of hurricanes hitting Barbados back in my great-grandparents' time, and they think that one big storm will wreck the island."

"Whereas," the crew member called Jacob remarked, "you all seem to be completely unfazed by the weather. It's as if this island is designed for climate change!"

"*Nei!*" I responded. "We're designed for North Atlantic weather! Which amounts to almost the same thing!"

We all laughed.

"Does it ever get sunny – do you have a summer?" Elise wanted to know, and that led to a long and often amusing discussion about heatwaves on En-Somi, the long hours of daylight, fishing through the night and the benefits of stone-built bothies.

Conversation only became serious when Jacob asked, "So this co-operative? How long has it been going? Do you export your stuff?"

"Hardly!" Sigrid explained. "There aren't enough of us. Tom sells some of our stuff down at the ferry port…"

"I knitted your *gensi*," I interrupted, smiling at Elise. "It was

85

one of last winter's projects – not this winter we're just coming out of, the winter before. My son had just gone off to Lerwick for school and I had more free time than I was used to."

"Marie is my star pupil," Sigrid told them. "She learnt a lot of what she knows when she arrived on En-Somi."

The Alba crew all looked surprised. "I thought you were an islander, born and bred!" Elise exclaimed. "You talk just like the other islanders!"

"*Nei*, I grew up on the mainland," I explained. "I've been here just over ten years."

"And will you ever go back?"

"Not a chance!" I answered, thinking of Malcolm. "This is home now."

"So, we talked to some of the people over near Storhaven," Ollie said. "This guy – Fin Murray – he was at the island council meeting, sort of chairing it – he asked us to dinner. He and his wife live in this really posh place. You might know it? In an area with a strange name."

"Floirean's Cnoc," put in Elise.

"Yeah, that's right. So, we went to dinner there, and they told us that this island is really quite backwards – reluctant to change. Stuck in its ways."

"He was really talking about you lot," Jacob said. "He called you peasants. We said we thought you are called *bondii*, but he said it was the same thing. He said that your continuous use of a dialect that's died out everywhere else just shows how unwilling the islanders are to change."

Sigrid laughed. "Well, point of order!" she exclaimed, looking amused. "Our dialect is unique. It hasn't died out everywhere else; it was never spoken on any other island!"

Elise wrinkled up her nose. "But aren't the Murrays islanders too?"

"Ah, well…" Sigrid gave a succinct and masterful account of the social structure of the island, the *bondii,* who are the ordinary people, and the *harkrav.* "The refugees call the *harkrav* 'the bosses'," Sigrid told the young people. "But really it means 'elites'. It comes from three words: *har krav pa,* which means 'the entitled ones'. Their families become entitled because they used to own a lot of the land; the *bondii* were mostly tenant farmers. During the land reforms they were forced either to work the land themselves or to give their tenants something called 'cultivation rights'. It meant that crofters who'd farmed the land for more than a certain period –"

"Fifty years," I put in.

"*Aja,* that's right," agreed Sigrid. "Fifty years. So, those families that had been tenants for fifty years or more no longer had to pay rents, as long as they didn't let the land go into disuse. Some of the properties on the land still belonged to the original owners, the *harkrav,* but a lot of the bothies were already owned by the *bondii.* The Scottish government paid the landowners compensation for losing rent, and the *harkrav* invested it wherever the wealthy make their investments. And of course, they don't have to pay taxes on that land now, either."

"So, the *bondii* don't own the land, but they're taxed on it?" Ollie had wrinkled up his nose, as if he thought it an odd arrangement.

"*Aja.* Well, we're only taxed on the land values, which are loosely based on the land's commercial possibilities; and as we mostly only grow what we need and don't expect to sell anything much, and as the officials who valued the land all those years ago recognised that ours is a subsistence economy, we hardly pay anything!" I explained.

"But the *harkrav* are still the rich ones on the island, and the *bondii* are poorer?" Elise was getting it clear in her mind.

"Well, richer than us!" I remarked.

"*Aja,* they're richer than us and with lots of connections in Edinburgh, London and Oslo." Sigrid paused a moment, frowning towards the *fi'ilsted* window, which had rain beating against it. "Are your bairns out on the moor?" she asked me. "They'll get a soaking today!"

"They'll be fine!" I reassured Sigrid. Then, "They send their children to private schools on the mainland," I continued. "To be honest, they've done some good for the island. It was them who first introduced the internet – that big mast over on Frigg Moor was their idea, and they like to be on the *Oyrod*, the island council. They get things done."

"Mm!" Sigrid wasn't impressed. "They get things done if it suits them," she said, which was true. "They like to be in charge. They think it's their right. But they live in a bubble – always mixing with each other. They live right alongside us, but they have no idea how we think!"

Ollie spoke slowly, as if he were thinking aloud. "I got the feeling that they don't really like you – the *bondii*. They need you here, on the island, to keep the place running – you know, fish in the summer, look after the sheep – but when they talked about you, they were… scornful, that's the best word I can think of."

Elise was frowning. "I thought that they were frightened of you. Like – as if you are some sort of unknown quantity. Unpredictable."

"Aye," Jacob agreed. "I would say that they think they know you. Or on one level they do. But then, they're not quite sure. When you brought down those arms dealers – they were all *harkrav*, weren't they? Well, they never expected that the *bondii* would do that."

Elise agreed. "And they never thought the islanders would be willing to keep the refugees," she added. "They're really upset about that. That guy Fin Murray, he said that you'd come to regret it. He said, 'Give them five years and they'll all have gone', and that you'll be the poorer for it."

Ollie added, "To be honest, I would say that's what they're hoping will happen, but I'm not sure that's what they really believe will be the outcome."

"They're mistaken, if that's what they're expecting," suggested Sigrid. She had a rather grim look on her face. "They're just thinking of their own pockets!"

"Can you explain that?" Jacob was in reporter mode.

"That's easy," I said. "The *harkrav* register most of their property and investments on the island because it gets them out of all sorts of taxes on the mainland, but if the refugees turn out to take a toll on the island economy, and taxes have to go up, they'll be the ones paying."

"But they can afford it!" maintained Sigrid.

Elise said, "You should have seen Fin Murray's house. Have you been there? It looked just like a large bothy on the outside – you know, single story, stone built, but inside…"

"It made me think of one of those trendy coffee shops in Edinburgh," interrupted Jacob. "Mood lighting, shiny surfaces, Japanese prints…"

"Aye, and several rooms," added Ollie. "So not at all like the other bothies we've seen since we came here."

"I quite liked it," Elise told us, "but not for this island. It would have been great as a holiday cottage, you know, a renovated crofters' cottage, somewhere in the highlands. Somewhere to go to celebrate a birthday, or to take a break…" Then she looked serious. "But I'll tell you what, if I were you, I'd be careful. I wouldn't trust those *harkrav* as far as I could throw them. They didn't invite us to dinner out of genuine hospitality. They wanted to know about our documentary – about what we're going to say. They wanted to put their own spin on island life."

"That was my impression too," Ollie agreed.

Jacob looked a little worried. "We've got to stay objective," he pointed out. "We shouldn't start taking sides."

"That's true," agreed Elise. "But we've got to be honest too. That Fin Murray thinks far too much of himself, and as for his wife…"

Sigrid laughed out loud then. "I've met his wife!" she

declared. "The least said, the better! Now, what can we tell you about island life? Marie ought to describe her arrival here – how she felt and what impressed her. Tell them about the goats grazing on the roof of the shop, Marie!"

The conversation moved on. The crew took out their recording equipment and I told them some of the funnier stories of my life on En-Somi, like the chickens being blown away, and some of my earlier attempts to speak the dialect. The mood lightened, but I didn't forget what the crew had told us. I would talk to Malcolm, I resolved, when he came to dinner that night. We needed to take into account *harkrav* opposition to the resettlement of the refugees, perhaps especially because now we were planning to renovate the bothy where we had camped while we were spying on the criminals. We were hoping that Charlie and his son Shawn might move in there, and Charlie had suggested that Mandy and her eleven-year-old might join them, to make up one household. That bothy is over on the east of the island, between St Matthew's Bay and Floirean's Cnoc, where the posh cottages are. They would be quite cut off from the rest of the refugees, and vulnerable. But vulnerable to what, I was not quite sure.

CHAPTER 10

Marigold was desperately upset that Duncan and Alana were going back to Shetland. The four bairns had become almost inseparable in a matter of days. When they weren't out and about on the island, they were in the Kullander's place or at mine. Duncan and Alana seemed to be the leaders of the group although Andy was the oldest. They had both spent time at school on Shetland; they knew about popular music and a bit about Scottish politics. Andy would normally have started school in Lerwick before the other two, but his uncertain health had kept him at home. Of the four, he was the most immersed in island culture. He could talk to Olaf in dialect with a fluency few of the other bairns could match, even using some of the archaisms that were dying out. Who needs words for 'invaders,' or 'fire-lighting flints' nowadays? They treated Marigold almost as if she were a mascot. They seemed to love showing her new things, explaining, describing, telling her stories, teaching her words. Without realising it, I saw, they were giving the wee lassie an accelerated education on island life. Under their tuition, Marigold flourished. Her speech started to change. Her confidence grew.

"I'll miss you!" she told the others. The four of them were sitting around the range in my bothy waiting for a batch of chocolate brownies to finish baking. These were to be supplies for Alana and Duncan to take to Shetland the next day.

"We'll be back in May," Alana pointed out.

"And in June, for the long holiday," added Duncan.

"Will you join us next year?" Alana asked Andy.

"I'm not sure… I'd rather stay here and study at home. I wonder what'd happen if I had an episode and I was away from Mam and Paps…"

"*Aja…*" Duncan was sympathetic. "But you wander all over En-Somi and nothing ever seems to happen."

"But you don't understand…" Andy sounded unhappy.

Marigold chipped in. "I'd rather you stayed 'ere," she told her friend. "If you goes too, I'll be on my own!"

"You know what, Marigold?" It was Duncan speaking again. "You ought to go to school here, in Hus. How old are you? Nine? Ten? So, then you could come to the Shetlands to school, too, in a couple of years. And if Andy could make it, all four of us'd be there for a few years. It would be such a laugh!"

Marigold looked uncertain. "You don't go to school nowhere!" she pointed out to Andy. "Why should I? Mum and Dad say school's dreadful. Like borstal… Any'ow, what's borstal?"

"I did go to the village school here in Hus," explained Andy. "I loved it. But now I do my lessons online and I have a tutor in Aberdeen who teaches a small group of us – a girl in Foula and a boy in Rum who has some sort of disability…"

"I think a borstal is a sort of prison," suggested Alana. "The village school isn't like that. Sigrid's nice – a bit strict, but friendly too."

"I think you have to go to school." Andy was sounding thoughtful. "It's the law."

"No, it ain't!" Marigold was certain. "I ain't never been to no school! Nor did Shawn, nor did Shirley, nor did Lavender… none of us 'as been to no school!"

Duncan put his arm round Marigold. He could tell that she was upset. "*Aja*, but then, your parents were working for nothing, for the *harkrav*, and that's against the law too! Now that you're free, I think you might have to have an education, just like everyone else."

"And there's some good kids in that school," insisted Andy. "Christian, he's my friend, and I'm sure you'd like Elin. She can make up songs and music… if I were you, I'd give it a go. And after school you could come up to my place, and I could help you if you had any problems."

"Or you could come to my mam! Mam! Marigold could ask you, if she started school in Hus and she didn't understand anything, couldn't she?"

"*Aja*, of course!" I was pleased with the direction the conversation had taken. "But I don't think Marigold's likely to have any difficulty! You're a very bright lassie!"

"What! Brighter than me?" Duncan sounded indignant.

I laughed. "Quite possibly! If Marigold goes to school, we'll soon find out!"

***

Malcolm and I took Duncan back to Storhaven for the Friday ferry. Marigold came with us, but Shona borrowed a pony trap from Robert in the village, because she was planning to stay the night with a cousin over on McGreggor Moor where the track leads down to the beach. Duncan chatted happily all the way across the island, but Marigold was unusually quiet.

There was the usual small crowd of secondary school-aged children and fraught-looking parents gathering at the ferry terminal. The boat was late because of the wind, but Tom assured everyone that it was on its way. Bairns exchanged tales of holiday activities, and the adults talked about the coming fishing season, the refugees and the failings of the *Oyrod*. It was after 2pm by the time the ferry arrived and the kids had boarded – nobody had got off, so the island had no new visitors. Then Malcolm and I took Marigold to Jeannie's café before the journey home.

It was when we were out of Storhaven, where the track is relatively flat before you reach the ruined chapel, that Marigold broke the silence. She was squeezed between Malcolm and me on the bench seat at the front of the cart.

"Does you think I should go to school?" she asked, and I noticed for the first time that she had pronounced the 'th' sound the way we do on the island, not as an 'f', the way the refugees often did.

Malcolm was cautious. "Sounds like a good idea," he said. "A bairn like you – I think you'd love it."

"*Aja!*" Marigold was obviously thinking it over. "Marie, that's what you thinks too, ain't it? But Mum and Dad…"

"Perhaps your mam and paps were sent to a different sort of school from ours?" Malcolm suggested. "I used to know some bairns in Edinburgh who hated school too. But I don't think they'd have hated Sigrid's lessons."

"Does you think that if I went to school, and I 'ated it, I could just stop going, like my dad did?"

"I think," Malcolm answered, with great conviction, "that if you went to school and you hated it, Marie and I would find out what the problem was, and we'd sort it out for you!"

The child sounded a little reassured. "Could you do that?"

"I'm sure we could!" I answered. "We wouldn't want you to be unhappy."

"I ain't un'appy!" Marigold told us. "I's 'appy as Larry." She thought for a moment. "Marie, 'o is Larry? And why is 'e so 'appy?"

Marigold invited us in when we got back to Hus. "Come an' see my mum and dad!" she suggested, then, slightly self-consciously, "my mam and paps."

"Are you sure?" I didn't want to invade the little family if they weren't really ready for visitors.

"*Aja!*" Marigold was insistent. "Mum – Mam – loves visitors. Shona comes in quite a lot, and Petter when 'e calls for Dad. Petter an' Dad's getting ready to 'elp over where that other bothy is, the one what Shawn will 'ave."

We were quite cold despite our warm jackets, and my first impression, going into the bothy, was how snug it all was. The range gleamed with a low, orange glow; the wall lights were on although it was still broad daylight outside, and Rose was sitting on the bottom bunk feeding Thistle, who seemed to have grown and changed every time I saw her.

"*Hei*, Mum!" Marigold sounded cheerful. "I's brought Marie and Malcolm in. Can I make some tea?"

Rose looked up from her bairn. "Of course, love," she said. "Excuse us, Thistle's as 'ungry as anything today!"

"No problem!" Malcolm was looking round. They still had no chairs although I recognised two of the little round stools from the *fi'ilsted*. "Anything I can do to help?" he asked Marigold, who was filling the kettle and finding mugs.

"Look!" Marigold was showing off. "We's got this kettle, and them things is tea bags. Andy's mam 'as 'em too, but Alana's mam says what loose leaf tea is better. And this thing – this kettle – it boils in no time, and it doesn't make no mess, or turn black on the outside!"

Rose was smiling. "All them things I took for granted when I were a kid," she said. "Marigold's learning them for the first time. Make us a brew, too, Marigold, will you? I's dying for a cuppa!"

Baby Thistle had gone to sleep. Rose put her down at the back of the bottom bunk where it was dark and took the mug offered to her by her daughter. "We 'ave all this food an' stuff," she told us. "Shona brings it over from the shop, but I don't know 'o pays for it or when we'll ever be able to pay 'em back."

"I think the government's paying," I answered. "You won't have to pay it back. It's just until you get on your feet."

Rose suddenly broke into a huge and unexpected smile. Her whole face lit up. "Me and Si," she told us, "we ain't never been on our feet! We always bin on our knees! If you 'ad told me, when I was a kid in Thamesmead in a mouldy council flat, that

one day I'd 'ave my own little 'ome, I'd never 'ave believed it!"
Her smile faded. Looking more thoughtful, she added, "It were
almost worth being a slave!"

"Was we really slaves?" Marigold wanted to know. Then,
"What's a slave?"

★★★

Si and Rose were worried about Marigold starting school, and
the bairn picked up on their anxiety. Sigrid went across and
talked to them and invited them to look around for themselves.
"It's not a bit like a city school," she reassured them. "Really, it's
just a place for the bairns to get together, to make friends, to learn
some useful things, and for us to find out what their strengths
are."

Sigrid told me about the conversation later.

"What if they don't 'ave no strengths?" Si had wondered.
"What if they's all weakness?"

"Well, I don't know," Sigrid had told them. "In all my
teaching career I've never come across a bairn who wasn't good
at something. Anyhow, that won't be your Marigold's problem!
She's as bright as a button, anyone can see that! And as for wee
Thistle – look at her, so alert already! I can tell you now that she's
going to be a joy to have in the classroom."

There was a slight problem registering Marigold. For one
thing, the birth of the refugee children on the island had never
been recorded anywhere. Officially, they didn't exist. Then,
too, Marigold had been nearer to the truth than we might have
expected, when she had said that her parents didn't have a last
name. Rose had been born to a single mother and raised by her
grandmother. "I fink she was called Mrs Kazinski," Rose had
told Sigrid, "and if my mum weren't married, I must be Rose
Kazinski. So, is Marigold, Marigold Kazinski?"

"Well…" Sigrid was very matter of fact about these things. "If you're marred to Si, then probably Marigold should have his last name, although it doesn't really matter."

"I ain't got no last name," Si had insisted.

"Well… what was your dad's last name?"

"No idea! Don't know 'o me dad was! Me mum lived wiv a bloke called Forester – Rube Forester, but 'e weren't me dad. She worked in a pub for a bloke called Stevie Evans. 'E might 'ave been me dad. And there was this geezer 'o came round sometimes, called somefing Carlton. 'E gave Mum money, so 'e might 'ave been me dad, or 'e might not…"

Sigrid admitted to me that she was knocked a bit off balance by these revelations. "So… what did they call you at school?" she had asked.

"Simon Smiff," Si had answered promptly. "But that weren't my name. That were just so no one'd come after anyone for money. You know, child support. But Smiff weren't my name, that's for sure."

"Right…" Sigrid had to think about this. "So, what did you give as your last name when Lyle had those forms to fill in?" she had asked.

"We just said what we had no last name and no number," Si said. "And Lyle, 'e just said not to worry and wrote somefing down and went away."

★★★

Lyle, bless him, had resolved the problem in his own way. The bothy had been in the hands of the Stewart family as far back as anyone could remember. On the official list required by the authorities, he had therefore given 'Stewart' as the family name. The fact that nobody in Edinburgh could trace a Si or Rose Stewart was just one of those things. There was altogether too much embarrassment about the mismanagement of the climate refugee problem for anyone there to query Lyle's findings.

Sigrid broke the news to the family when they were in the *fi'ilsted* at Malchi's invitation that Saturday. "You've been given a family name," she had told them. "So that we can register Marigold in the school. You're officially Si and Rose Stewart now!"

Apparently, Si had looked amazed. "We sounds like we belong 'ere!" was his response.

"Both of us?" Rose had wanted to know. "Both of us is Stewart, even though we isn't really married? Like, not in a church or a' office?"

"Well," was Sigrid's common-sense response, "you are in a way, aren't you? And who's to know? Or care?"

CHAPTER 11

It was a couple of days later, and I was on my own at home. That was quite unusual. Malcolm and I had developed a sort of pattern to our lives. Either I was at his place, or he was at mine. After Duncan went back to school, though, I had more than the usual amount of cleaning and laundry to do, and Malcolm had been busy applying for all the necessary permissions to renovate the bothy over towards St Matthew's Bay.

I suppose it was about eight in the evening and the sun was just dropping below the horizon, leaving behind streaks of red and gold in the sky. I remember that I was feeling good. Si and Rose seemed to be settling well; Duncan had been happy to go back to school; Malcolm was a calm, warm presence in my life. I felt an overwhelming sense of gratitude as I watched the sky darken and saw the first, bright star appear.

Then the phone rang.

It was Verity. "*Hei*, Marie!"

"*Hei*, Verity. How's it going?"

At the other end Verity paused, then, "Well... good, I think." There was hesitation in her voice. "Holti is being wonderful, and the Frasers... and it really helps having the BBC Alba people here, because they're never taken in by the *harkrav*! That Elise, especially – she asks the most awkward questions, all in the name of accurate reporting, and she isn't fooled if Munro or Murray try to fob her off. But..."

I waited a moment or two for Verity to finish her sentence, but she had stalled.

"Do you want to come over?" I asked. "You've been pretty busy recently. Do you even take a day off? Come and have dinner. Would you like it to be just us, or shall I invite Malcolm too?"

There was a short pause, then, "Oh, I'd love that! And yes, please invite Malcolm too. But not Lyle. Would that be all right?"

Interesting! I thought, and phoned Malcolm to make the arrangements.

★★★

Verity took Mondays and Tuesdays off. Obviously, she worked on Sundays, and she told us that Saturdays were often her busiest days. "I don't know why," she wondered. "It's not as if anyone much works Mondays to Fridays on the island!"

It was for the following Monday evening that we had arranged the dinner. I was doing a roast, and Malcolm was bringing home-made ice-cream. Verity arrived before Malcolm, and we were standing outside looking out to sea when Malcolm arrived. He went in to put the pudding in the fridge and came back out to stand beside us.

There is something special about the light in the late afternoons in April. The weak sun seems to hang high in the sky, and the stacks over beyond Michaelmas Fjell make dark shadows in the sea. That day there were high clouds, grey and blue-tinted, and whenever the sun came out from behind them the sea sparkled. We seemed to be able to see a long way, to a dark shadow right on the horizon.

"Is that Liten Stein?" Verity wanted to know.

"I don't think so. I've often wondered," I told her.

"Could just be some sort of illusion," suggested Malcolm.

"They say that on a really clear day you can see the island," I pointed out.

"They say that on a really clear night you can see the lights of Porkeri on the Faroe Islands!" laughed Malcolm. "But I don't believe it for a minute! Is it too early for a wee glass of something, do you think?"

We chatted about various things while I worked in the kitchen and the other two watched me and sipped their whiskies. Some of the Storhaven people had really rallied round Lyle, Holti and the Frasers, as they started to organise the next renovation. The McGreggor Moor Sinclairs claimed ownership of that bothy, but as they had very little land so far to the east of the island, they were happy to have refugees living there. Meanwhile Yanni Sinclair, second cousin to the McGreggor Moor Sinclairs, and much better known to us because he lived in the west of the island, had started the onerous task of carting stones from the bothy destroyed by the sea down by the summer harbour, up onto the moorland west of Norse Hill. Verity hoped that two adults and two bairns would live there.

"A family?" Malcolm asked. We felt that we knew some of the refugees quite well, but others were just tired faces that we had seen around smoky fires or holding *harkrav* villains at bay with grim and determined expressions on their faces.

"Well… *nei*. None of the refugees seem to be whole families," Verity told us. "Only Si and Rose. It's hard to make sense of it. It seems people got separated from each other, in floods or avalanches or in the endless movements from one camp to another… and then, over the years that they were enslaved, there seem to have been a few liaisons. There's a woman called Mandy, with a young daughter. Do you remember? I think she's the mother of an older boy too, but I'm not sure – and the tall, quiet man with the squint, he wants to set up home with them. I worry about them. It's one thing to live all together, like a tribe, quite another to live like a nuclear family, miles from other people… what if they don't get on?"

"Well, they've known each other long enough," I pointed out. "Ten years living out at the old airport. They're hardly rushing into anything!"

"I can see why you're concerned, though," Malcolm was sympathetic. "But we're not going to abandon them, once they've moved in. We'll just have to deal with issues as they arise – if they arise."

Verity sighed. "*Aja*. Anyhow," she added, "that's the least of my problems."

"Oh dear," said Malcolm, encouragingly. "You really didn't arrive on En-Somi at a very peaceful time! Can we help?"

"I don't think so." Verity was whirling her whisky round in her glass so that it caught a stream of sunlight that came in through one of my west-facing windows. "But it might help to talk."

"Go on!" Malcolm's voice was gentle.

Verity sighed again. "I don't really know where to start," she told us.

"Lyle?" I prompted.

"*Aja!*" She looked up at me and smiled. "I knew you would have guessed. He wants to marry me."

"Is that a problem?" I had thought that Verity had seemed as attached to Lyle as he was to her.

"No…" Verity was obviously unsure. "Well, you know, I'm the minister of the kirk."

"Is there a rule that the minister of the kirk mustn't be married to a *nasyoni*?" asked Malcolm, mildly.

Verity laughed. "*Nei* – no! Of course not. But – if the elders ask me to leave, I might have to go somewhere else, to some other parish. A different island or the mainland. And Lyle wants to stay here."

Malcolm stood up and went across to the table. Without saying anything he poured more whisky into Verity's glass and his own and raised a questioning eyebrow to me. I shook my head *nei* and he returned to his seat.

"Do you think the elders are likely to want you to go?" I asked.

Verity was silent for a few minutes. I thought perhaps she wasn't going to answer, but then she said, "Perhaps. I don't know. When I arrived most of the congregation was *harkrav*. I'm pretty sure most of them would like me to go now. They don't like the kirk being used to house and feed the refugees until we can settle them somewhere permanently. And you know, that's going to take time. But in the last month or so, since all this business with the arms traders, well... more *bondii* are there on Sundays now. And some of the refugees themselves. Numbers have gone up."

"It doesn't sound to me as if you'll be asked to leave," Malcolm offered.

"Well, but the thing is..." Again, Verity stopped without finishing her sentence.

And then I guessed what the problem was. "Do you think, maybe, that you no longer want to be the minister?" I asked.

Malcolm looked sharply at me, surprised, but Verity nodded.

"Yes, *aja*," she said and sipped her whisky. "That's it, Marie. I ought to be really happy to see all those people in the pews. You know, it's a mark of a successful ministry, isn't it? Numbers going up, members of the kirk actively involved in the community. But I don't think I can lead them the way I should."

Neither of us spoke. After a little more silence, Verity got to the heart of the matter. "I don't quite believe it all, anymore..." she told us. "Or *nei* – I believe it, but I don't see it the same. Does that make sense? The minister is officially the teaching elder, but I don't even think there should be a teaching elder! I'm beginning to think that God can teach people through anyone."

"You sound like a Quaker," Malcolm said.

Verity gave a weak smile. "*Aja*, well... I've been reading all this stuff about the Quakers. I'm beginning to think that's where I belong." She gulped the last of her whisky. "And there aren't any Quakers on En-Somi."

"If you became one, there would be," pointed out Malcolm. "Perhaps that's just what the island needs." He was quiet for a moment. "I might join you," he added, "then there'd be two of us."

CHAPTER 12

I think the thing that swayed Rose, so that she encouraged Marigold to try school, was the fact that our village children didn't wear any sort of uniform. They still don't, of course. Lyle told me that there had been a time, years and years earlier, when attempts had been made to convince the parents to follow the practice of the mainland, for the bairns to wear, at the very least, sweatshirts or hoodies with the 'Gamla Hus Primary' logo printed on the back. The idea never took off. We were not then, and we're not now, much of a cash economy, although of course we do use some money. Almost all the islanders wear hand-knitted *gensii* for three quarters of the year, and the comparatively lightweight, fleecy garments that arrived as samples for the parents to look at seemed flimsy and unsubstantial to the *bondii* on our side of the island. To Si and Rose, who had been dressed in standard uniforms from the day they first entered their school buildings, the fact that our bairns arrived at their classes dressed in the clothes their parents thought most fitting was the proof and reassurance they needed that Marigold was not going to suffer as they had.

Marigold herself approached this new development in her life with interest but not, it seemed to me, with the sort of excitement I had seen in Duncan as he approached his first day in school.

"What if I needs to ask a question?" the bairn wanted to know, as I measured her up for a new *gensi*. She had been wearing a cast-off of mine on and off ever since the family moved to Hus, but it was too big, and looked like a tunic on her, and the plan was to pass it on to Rose when I had knitted a new one for Marigold.

"You just put up your hand," I said, demonstrating, "and wait until Sigrid calls on you."

"But..." Marigold screwed up her face, thinking hard. "What if I forgets to put up my 'and? What if I just says, 'Sigrid, I doesn't understand'?"

"Well then," I answered, "I think Sigrid will probably answer your question and then say 'Try to remember to put up your hand, Marigold.'"

"Dad says – I mean Paps – that if you don't put up your 'and, the teacher says, 'Shut up! Speak when you's spoken to!'"

I laughed. "I really can't imagine Sigrid saying that!" I reassured her.

"But what if I as 'iccups, or burps, or yawns?" the child persisted. "Mam says what they makes you go and stand in a corner and puts a frowning face next to your name, on a chart, for being rude. And then at playtime the other kids calls you names. And if you cries, they call you a cry-baby."

"I think," I told Marigold, "that perhaps your mam and paps went to very different sorts of schools from the one here in Hus. Has Andy ever mentioned name-calling, when he's told you about going to school?"

"*Nei*," the child answered. "But you know, Marie, Andy belongs 'ere. 'E ain't no refugee what used to be a slave. 'E ain't no *sommy klinger*."

Then I gave the bairn a big hug. "You're no stranger to En-Somi," I told her. "You're Marigold Stewart, born and bred on this island! And *sommy klinger* are unkind words; I would really like it if I never heard you say them again!"

The child clung on to me and said into my shoulder, "Sometimes, Marie, I doesn't know 'o I am. Marigold Stewart – that sounds like someone else. I's just Marigold, really, ain't I?"

"You'll always be Marigold," I reassured her. "A very special girl, with a very special baby sister and very special parents. Whatever adventures you have in this life, you'll always be Marigold."

"You forgot about Lavender!" the lassie reminded me. "She was very special too!"

"Of course she was!" I agreed.

★★★

I was given two accounts of Marigold's first day at school. She came to see me almost as soon as the school day was over, running down the track to my bothy and calling out, "Marie! Marie! I done it! I went to school!"

"Well done!" I answered, giving the bairn a hug. "Have you told your mam all about it?"

"*Aja!*" She was hopping up and down in excitement. "I left my backpack in the 'ouse and Mam said what I could come and see you!"

"So, what happened?" I asked, taking down the biscuit tin.

Marigold plonked herself onto one of the rocking chairs and started rocking energetically back and forth. "I was so good an' quiet!" she announced. "I sat where Sigrid told me and I listened 'ard, and I watched what the other children did, and I waited to answer questions, and I didn't say no bad words, and Sigrid smiled at me, and nobody called me names, and that wee girl Elin what's a cousin to Lyle, she taught us a song with strange words what I didn't understand, and there's two twins but one is a boy and one is a girl, and did you know what there are odd and even numbers?"

"Goodness me!" I was really amused. "It sounds like quite a day."

Marigold took one of the proffered biscuits. "*Aja!*" she agreed. "A busy day, but I was as quiet as a mouse." She thought for a moment. "Marie, is mice quiet?"

Sigrid's version only contradicted Marigold's on one point. "That child never stops asking questions!" she told me, smiling. "I've never taught a bairn like her!"

We were talking in the village shop, where I was picking up some post for Malcolm and me, and where Sigrid was putting up a handmade poster about a pupils' art exhibition which the school was planning.

"Did she behave?" I wanted to know. "Did she make friends?"

"Well..." Sigrid was, of course, a professional. "It's early days for making real friends. It helps that she knows Andy Kullander, because Andy and Christian are such good friends. Christian did a good job of taking Marigold under his wing. Little Elin hung around Marigold at break, but I think she was just interested in the way the bairn speaks. Elin has a good ear for speech patterns. Some of the children wanted to know if Marigold was a cousin to Hamish Stewart – Paula and Robbie's little one. Most of the Stewarts on En-Somi are related, after all."

I laughed. "How did Marigold handle that one?" I wondered.

"Pretty well. She just said, 'I ain't no cousin to nobody!' and then asked who was related to whom in the school. That kept them going for quite a while!"

★★★

Si had started to go over to St Matthew's Bay with Malcolm, to work on the renovations of that bothy and, when time allowed, to plant small potato and kale beds. The new inhabitants of the bothy would need to begin as they would have to go on if they were going to survive on the island. Although the place had seemed to be in a reasonable condition when Lyle, Verity, Malcolm and I had camped out in it, during our campaign to bring down the arms traders, it seemed that there were a few problems beyond broken windows and out-of-date heating which depended on open fires. There was a drainage problem, to do with a patch of land higher up on the moors behind the bothy where in the past there had been some quite extensive peat digging, and before much more could be done to the bothy, the old peat bog needed to be drained away from the building. Several people from Storhaven were helping with the work too, and the refugee Charlie and his son Shawn were already camping out in the ruin and helping in every way they could. It meant that, with Marigold at school, Rose was left alone all day in their bothy with baby Thistle.

"Come and have lunch!" I suggested when I popped in. "I'd love to get to know Thistle better. And you, of course!"

They arrived one windy morning about a week after Marigold had started school. Fiona Kullander had volunteered to give Marigold her tea so that Rose didn't have to hurry back. Rose was carrying the baby in a sling made of knotted rope, the little one all wrapped up in a tartan blanket and looking wide awake.

"Can I put 'er on the ground?" Rose wanted to know, looking around. "She's started to want to crawl! Look!"

She placed the wee girl on the floor behind the rocking chairs, close to my bookcase. Thistle gurgled approvingly and dribbled onto the slates. With her knees pulled up under her, she made a sort of shuffling movement and progressed perhaps five inches towards the bottom row of books.

"Oh, that's great!" The progress of babies never ceases to amaze me. "How old is she? Eight months?"

"Seven," Rose told me, looking proudly at the child. "Born last August. Not a day I'll quickly forget. Fought I was going to die…"

"It's a tough business," I agreed, "giving birth on the island. I went across to Shetland for Duncan's birth. Sigrid and Bjorn went with me. How did you manage?"

"Not well." Rose had swivelled one of the rocking chairs around, so that she could watch the uncertain progress of the baby. "If it 'adn't been for Frankie… them bosses, they said what the nurse would come over, but she never did come. They didn't want no babies around, you see. But Frankie, she 'elped me. I bled a lot. More'n I did with any of the uvers… but Frankie, she said what she bled that much with Shirley's aunty, 'er what was married to Eric, the one what died in the floods, and she just 'ad to 'ave bed rest. So, I just stayed by the fire for a week, and I mended. But I 'urt for ages."

"Tea or coffee?" I offered. "Obviously you had all your children out here, on the island?"

"Yeah… Marigold and Lavender, what you knows about, and a little boy what didn't come out alive and a miscarriage and Thistle. I don't want no more. They breaks your 'eart."

I wondered if Rose knew about family planning and who the nurse was who didn't come out to help with Thistle's birth. Back then there was no doctor on the island and only one practising nurse, but it occurred to me that it wouldn't have been him. We depended on Shetland for most of our healthcare and all of our dentistry, a situation which was becoming increasingly precarious as the weather became more extreme and the island was cut off so often.

"I'm so sorry," I commiserated. "To lose three children…"

"Yeah." Rose was watching the baby still, not looking at me. "But there's uvers what've 'ad it worse."

"I'm not sure that helps…"

Rose turned then and looked at me. "It does 'elp!" she insisted. "I finks of them people on Thamesmead when the floods came and 'ow many of them just didn't make it, and I finks what I 'ave Si an' Marigold an' Thistle, and now I 'as a last name and an 'ouse what's called a bothy… yeah, it 'elps to remember uver people!"

Then, to my surprise, she changed the subject. "Marie," she suggested, "if you wanted, I could make a 'ammock to put up

110

there –" she pointed to the place beside my sleeping platform, next to the floor-to-ceiling bookcase. "You could put winter stuff up there in the summer, an' summer stuff up there in the winter." Then she looked doubtful. "If you wants to," she added.

"Oh Rose, could you?" I had seen the storage hammocks in their bothy. "It would be so useful."

"I'd like to," she told me. "I learnt to tie them knots – it's called macramé – at one of them classes they gives to refugees in the camps. You know, so's we 'ave somefing to do. People wiv posh voices comes in to teach you stuff. Uver people made them 'anging baskets for plants, but I fought, I don't want no plants, I wants somewhere to put me stuff, so I used the knots to make 'ammocks. It were the only useful fing I ever learnt in them camps! Then Si, 'e says, "Will you make one for me?' We was in the same camp, you see, but I didn't know 'im yet. So I made 'im one, and then 'im and me, we got together. And then they sent us up 'ere."

I tried to imagine what Rose's life had been like, but I really couldn't. Some people thought I had had it tough, losing both my parents at such a young age, but compared with Rose…

I made tea and we drank it in companionable silence, until Thistle had had enough of shuffling around on the floor and started to grumble. Then Rose fed her, and we played with her and put her down for her rest on the settle. I realised that this lovely wee one was the third of the Stewart siblings to sleep on my settle, and I felt grateful.

Rose stayed until well into the evening, when Malcolm returned and told us that Si had found his bothy empty and was eating his dinner in the *fi'ilsted*.

CHAPTER 13

For a week or two, the way I remember it, time seemed to pass relatively uneventfully. Malcolm was away for long days, over at the St Matthew's Bay bothy with Si, working on the renovations there. Sometimes both men stayed the night at the Frasers, where the Alba film crew was also lodging, so it must have been quite a gathering! More often than not, though, Si came home, arriving late and, so Rose told me, "starving 'ungry!" When Si was away, Rose and her two girls often ate their evening meal with Shona and Patrick at the shop. A few times, if Shona was busy (she was making goat's cheese, I think I recall) then Rose would mind the store, although she was a little challenged when it came to handling the money. Still, it meant that she was getting to know the Gamla Hus people.

I remember being there once when Olaf had wandered in. It wasn't usual to see him in the shop. He was one of the old folk, those islanders who liked, as far as possible, to be entirely self-sufficient. It was rare to see him buying chocolate, for instance, or tins of baked beans, and I doubt if he had much post to collect. Still, there he was, leaning on the rather cluttered counter next to the till and laughing with Rose about something.

As I came in, Rose was saying, "… So we just put it all in together and added them spuds with the purple bits in them and called it Scottish stew. But we didn't know nofing about Scottish food!"

Olaf answered, "Well, you're certainly learning now, Rose Stewart! When the fishing starts properly, we'll teach you how to make fish stew, then you'll be one of us in every way!"

Rose blushed, smiled and said, "*Aja!*"

When Olaf had left, Rose said to me, "They all calls me 'Rose Stewart', them old people. Not just 'Rose', always 'Rose Stewart'. But you and Malcolm, you still calls me 'Rose'... and uver people, they doesn't use no last names. So why do they do that? Call me 'Rose Stewart' I mean?"

"They're telling you that you belong," I explained. "In the old days, when a lassie married and changed her name to her husband's name, the custom was always to address the new bride by both her names for a while. It was a sort of affirmation – a way of telling her that her new status was recognised. Most people don't do that now, but Olaf does things the traditional way. He's letting you know that you're accepted into the community."

Rose smiled slowly and was quiet for a moment or two. Then, "Sometimes I can't quite believe what this is me," she confessed. "I wakes up in the night, and I lies there, feeling clean and warm, and there's rain on the window and wind in the chimney, and I finks, *I's in En-Somi in a 'ouse of me own*, and I tries to remember what it were like living in that old airport, or in the camps, and it all feels like a dream. And I finks 'ow my little Lavender would 'ave loved it. And it makes me sad..."

★★★

During those few weeks Marigold also appeared to be settling well. She seemed to mix easily enough with the other children, although Sigrid told me that she had to rescue the bairn once or twice, when other children asked her awkward questions. It was not surprising, given that there must have been talk among the adults about the refugees, in bothies and in the *fi'ilsted*, so the youngsters came into school wanting to know more. Sigrid told me that she came across a conversation about slavery. The older bairns had been learning about the Caribbean slave plantations, and Marigold was inundated by questions about beatings and overseers and children being sold away from their parents. The lassie obviously didn't know how to explain. She just kept saying, "But it weren't like that!" until Sigrid stepped in and explained that, although there is generally only one way of doing the right thing, there are millions of ways of doing wrong.

"People have enslaved other people all over the world, since the beginning of time," she had told the little group of children. "Some of our ancestors probably went to the Caribbean and mistreated the slaves there. We should never forget that. But Marigold was a different sort of slave."

"Yeah – *aja!*" Marigold had confirmed, looking relieved. "There weren't no beatings, except that one time when Charlie told the bosses 'e'd go to Stor'aven and tell everyone what we didn't 'ave enough to eat. Just swearing and calling us names what Marie says I shouldn't say, and them bosses telling us that if we didn't do what we was told, they would 'ave us all sent back to the camps."

"My mam says it's wrong to threaten people," Elin had declared.

"*Aja,*" Christian had agreed. "The *harkrav* did a bad thing, making you slaves. It's frightening, thinking there are bad men on En-Somi." The lad was oversensitive in those days. "By the way, did you learn how to play jacks over there? We could teach you now!"

And so these awkward moments passed.

★★★

It must have been late April when I first noticed that Marigold was struggling. Sigrid and I had set aside a weekend for planting our potatoes – like most people on the island we grow Shetland Blacks, which are really more purple than black, and I had also been preparing my kale beds. We grow our kale in small, circular, walled fields – we call them *gronnki sengi* which I'm sure comes from the Norwegian originally. Kale is more or less a staple on En-Somi, even more so now than then, because the storms have made importing food so unpredictable. There is a lot one can do with kale.

Marigold had walked down to visit me after school. I showed her a picture of what the kale would look like when it was grown, and we talked a little about food values. Sigrid had been teaching the children about proteins and vitamins, and Marigold was fascinated with her new knowledge that by choosing what to eat we can control, to some extent, our own growth and health. I grew Red Russian kale in those days; it makes such good salad. We *En-Som-in-Fedii* use kale in most of our recipes, either raw or cooked.

"Why is vegetables purple 'ere?" Marigold wanted to know.

I was rather surprised. "Well, they're not!" was my answer. "Kale is green a lot of the time; my kale just grows purple at certain times. Later in the year, if you're up at the Kullanders', take a look at Fiona's vegetable garden. She grows lettuces which are green and tomatoes which are red…"

"But…" the bairn was frowning. "'Ere fings is often purple. Our onions 'ave purple skins and our spuds is purple. Mum and Dad – I mean Mam and Paps – they say what they never seen purple spuds before. The ones in the camps was white, or black if they was going bad. When they first saw spuds wiv purple rings in 'em, they fought what they was rotten."

"Ah, but you know better now!" I suggested. "I heard that your paps has started planting his own potatoes, behind your bothy? Did you help him?"

Marigold perched on the big rock that marks the narrow entry to my kale field. She stared away from me, out at the rough, grey sea.

"I 'elped Paps," she agreed. "In the school all the bairns 'elps their mams and paps. But my mam and paps, they ain't like other people's. We's foreigners, really. We's called 'Stewarts' but we ain't really, properly, Stewarts. We's really, properly, nobodies."

I stood to stretch my back but stayed quiet. The child was troubled, and I wanted her to be free to say whatever she wanted to say, without any prompting from me.

"I wish I 'ad cousins 'ere," she added, still staring out at the hazy, grey horizon. "I's the only person in the school with no cousins. I didn't even know about cousins until I come 'ere. Dad – Paps – 'e said 'e 'ad cousins once, only they got lost after Withernsea got flooded. I feels like my world 'as got bigger, and I's got smaller. Like I's just floating around, not connected to no one. And, Marie, where's Withernsea?"

★★★

Then Rose confided her concerns about Marigold. We were sitting in Sigrid's bothy by the school. Sigrid and I were knitting, and Rose was knotting hammocks. Thistle was sitting at Rose's feet, chewing a wooden doll that Olaf had made for her.

"She's sad," Rose told us. "I 'ears 'er crying at night, but when Si or me asks 'er, she says she's fine."

"She seems all right at school," Sigrid reassured her. "She isn't being bullied or left out. The other bairns have taken to her – she always has someone to play with. And she works hard. She's pretty much caught up with the others when it comes to reading, and her writing will follow soon, I'm sure. Although spelling doesn't seem to be her strong point!"

Rose gave a worried smile. "Well, no," she agreed. "Si and me, we never could spell nofing!"

"She's had a lot to deal with in these last few months," I suggested. "Think of all the changes in her life! Six months ago, she was one of a settled group over at the old airport, seeing the same people every day, and she didn't know anything else."

"Yeah, *aja.*" Rose agreed. "But fings 'ave got better for 'er, not worse. I doesn't know why she ain't 'appy." She frowned again. "Si and me, we's 'appy, and Thistle – look at 'er! –'appy as any baby ever was! But Marigold, she cries in 'er bed at night, and then she tells us she don't... I doesn't know what to do."

"Maybe just give her time?" Sigrid suggested. "And lots of love."

"Per'aps." Rose didn't sound convinced. Then, "Marie, will you talk to 'er? Try to find out what's the matter? She likes you."

"I'll certainly try," I agreed.

CHAPTER 14

Malcolm and I were sitting in my two rocking chairs, drawn up close to the range. We were nursing small glasses of Malcolm's favourite whisky, after eating rather too much of his special Irish stew concoction. It was about 9pm. The sun was setting in a blaze of red and gold so that my west-facing windows looked almost like stained glass. Despite my triple glazing, we could hear the long, drawn-out calls and the *kek kek* of black-backed gulls defending their territory. Malcolm had been away for several days, working over at the St Matthew's Bay bothy, but was back for a week or more, intending to work his own land.

"I had a long talk with Lyle yesterday," he told me.

"How's he doing?" I wanted to know. We saw little of the *nasyoni* in the village nowadays – he was busy over at Storhaven, dealing with all sorts of complications caused by the refugees and the pending criminal case involving the arms dealers.

"I think he's finding life tough," Malcolm told me. "Despite everything the Alba crew are doing to call them to count, the *Oyrod*, the island council, is being obstructive. Well, not all of them, of course. And when it comes to the group who enslaved our refugees, there's some sort of big-wig lawyer on the mainland, trying to put the blame for the treatment of the refugees on Holyrood or Westminster, painting our *harkrav* as well-meaning entrepreneurs who were just trying to create livelihoods for people abandoned by the authorities. It won't wash, of course, but it's a delaying tactic. The idea is to slow everything up until the media storm has died down, then the *harkrav* will use their influence to obtain light sentences – or even get their cases dismissed. You know, they'll give generous donations to the appropriate political party, and the problem will just go away."

"Poor Lyle," I commiserated. "You wouldn't expect to start out on a career as a *nasyoni* in a small village and end up dealing with these sorts of shenanigans, would you?"

Malcolm smiled and sipped his whisky. "I think he's quite good at it all," he added. "He keeps his cool. He's got his head screwed on. I expect if everything else in his life was going smoothly, he would be fine."

"Everything else in his life isn't going smoothly?" I prompted, although of course I had a pretty good idea of what Malcolm was about to say.

"He's pining for Verity," Malcolm told me. "That young laddie is head over heels in love, but she's holding back. Well, you know what she told us. He's moved out of her flat – he's been dossing in that box room since all this started, whenever he was in Storhaven, but it's more than either of them can cope with, the way things are now."

"Oh dear!" It was hard for me to imagine the strain there must have been between these two dear friends of ours.

"And he can see that Verity is in trouble," added Malcolm. "She isn't happy. She's working her socks off, organising programmes for the refugees, helping them to cope until their bothies are ready and trying to keep things easy between the Storhaven residents and the incomers. She ought to be in her element, but Lyle can see as well as I can that Verity's struggling with her faith. And Lyle – well, how can he help with that? It's not something he ever gave much thought to, until he met her."

"So, there they both are," I summed up, "pining for each other, feeling unable to get together and both working flat-out for other people."

"Exactly," Malcolm agreed.

119

"What can we do?" I wondered.

Malcolm swirled the last of his whisky round in his glass. Outside, the sun dipped below the horizon and suddenly my bothy was all in shadow. Malcolm downed the last of his drink and put his glass on the floor at his feet. He reached out and took my hand.

"I don't want to shock you," he said, "but I've been thinking. Do you remember that night when we were locked in the shed, and Lyle was so poorly, and we had no idea how we were going to get out?"

I held his hand tightly. How could I ever forget? "I remember," I said.

"And you were sitting over by the door. Do you remember what you did?"

"I prayed," I replied. "Well, sort of. I did what Verity had talked about and just lifted the whole situation up to the Light."

"Mm." Malcolm's hand was rough and warm in mine. I almost felt as if I were there again, next to the two men in the dark, with a storm raging outside. "So, I'm thinking, that's what we need to do now. Life's too complicated for us to work everything out. We need help."

"A higher power," I said, remembering back to a friend in my university days.

Malcolm continued to hold my hand tight. He closed his eyes. Suddenly I felt as if he had gone away from me. I wanted to join him, to be where he was. I closed my eyes too. I pictured the setting sun. I heard the gulls, distantly, outside. And I felt that we were together again, and I knew that we were doing the right thing. I didn't hear – or feel – a voice, the way I had in that shed, but I felt a sense of peace. In fact, I felt a sense of completion. If you pressed me, I would say that it was in that moment that the situation was resolved, somewhere in some sphere we don't understand, although it took months for us to see the outcome.

When we made love, that night, it was slower and somehow

more luxurious than ever before. We had found a new closeness, an extra dimension to our relationship. I dreamt about Granny, but she wasn't in Melrose anymore. She was here, on En-Somi, baking scones and humming to herself. She looked younger than I remember her, and more carefree.

★★★

It wasn't hard to find time with Marigold. I had told Malcolm, of course, about Rose's concern, and her request to me, so when Marigold turned up at my bothy a day or two later, and found Malcolm and me sitting on my stone bench looking out to sea and drinking tea, he quickly made an excuse and left.

"I think I'll just go down to your beach, if that's okay, Marie?" he announced. "I want to see if there's any driftwood we can carve into pegs to hang coats on, over at Charlie's bothy." He grinned conspiratorially at us both as Marigold sat beside me, swinging her legs. "We're trying not to buy anything we can make for ourselves, to save all the money for taxes!"

We both watched him as he passed my storehouse and turned the corner, following the steep path down to the sea.

"That's where you found my Lavender," Marigold said. Her voice was sad. It wasn't a question; it was more as if she were thinking aloud.

"*Aja*," I agreed.

"But she weren't dead yet," the bairn continued. "And you brung 'er up 'ere, to your 'ouse, and you tried to warm 'er up, but you couldn't. And she died."

"*Aja*," I replied. "How do you know all that?"

"Lyle told me. 'E said what you did everything what a 'uman being could do."

"I hope I did," I responded.

"Did you cry?" she wanted to know. "When she died, did you cry?"

"Yes, I did." I felt as if I were reassuring her. Surely, everyone should cry when a child dies?

"That were the night she were washed into the sea," Marigold continued.

"*Aja*, it must have been." I thought, but didn't say, that nobody could last in that bitter cold water for more than an hour or so. It was amazing that she had any breath left in her body when I found her.

"I watched 'er go," Marigold told me. "We was all on the beach. We 'ad to go out, even though it were so stormy, because we 'ad to deliver them drone things. If we didn't 'and 'em over, they'd be no new food. Them bosses 'ad gone, and we was going to walk 'ome by the road, because the sea 'ad got so rough. She were just standing by me. Then this big wave came in – it were bigger than me – and it crashed over us both, and I stepped back and Jarvis caught me, and 'e couldn't reach Lavender, and she were gone, out in the water. Just gone."

We were both quiet. I wondered if the bairn had ever told anyone about the incident, anyone who hadn't been there. I guessed not.

"I wish what Jarvis 'ad saved Lavender, instead of me," the child added. "She were prettier than me. She loved Thistle."

What could I say? How do you begin to comfort a child who has experienced such trauma?

We were both quiet again. A gull landed on a rock by my kale enclosure and looked at us both, his head on one side, then squawked and flew off.

"They all tried to save 'er," the bairn continued. "Jarvis, 'e dived in under the next wave. I 'adn't never seen nobody do that before. But 'e couldn't reach 'er. And Frankie and Charlie and all them – they all waded in, but the sea sort of sucked 'er out, away from us. And Jarvis started swimming in them big waves, but Frankie called out to 'im to come back, because it weren't no use. She were gone. It were dark, you see, and you couldn't see 'er no more."

Just at that moment, Malcolm returned. He had several stout pieces of wood under one arm. He took one look at us and announced, "I'm going inside, if that's okay with you two. Would you like some more tea?"

When the door was closed on him, the silence continued. I wondered if the child had more to say.

"It sounds as if Jarvis did his best," I suggested.

"*Aja.*" Marigold looked thoughtful. "I doesn't usually like Jarvis, 'cos 'e's strange, but that night... if 'e could 'ave saved Lavender, 'e would 'ave."

We were quiet again. Then, "In the end, you saved 'er."

"No," I answered sadly. "I couldn't save her. I found her, but she was too cold. She'd been in that sea for ages, tossed this way and that. People aren't designed to survive that sort of thing."

Marigold continued to stare out to sea.

"If she 'ad lived," she told me, "I wouldn't care what I 'ad no cousins." A frown appeared on her face. "I don't never talk about 'er, you know. I mean about Lavender. I pretends what I always just 'ad one sister, baby Thistle. I feels like, if the other bairns knew, it would be like they could see too much of me, as if I went to school with no cloves on. It ain't their business. Nor I don't talk to Mam and Paps, 'cos they would be sad too. I just thinks about 'er and wishes she were 'ere."

I thought to myself that probably all the schoolchildren knew about Lavender's death, and that the wee bairn had been Marigold's sister. In a small community like ours, there are few secrets. I was aware, from something Lyle had told me, that young Christian had become very anxious about the thought of a child being washed up on my beach. He was always a sensitive child. I guessed that parents had warned their young ones not to talk about it at school, both for Marigold's and for Christian's sake.

Again, we were quiet. "So, what did you do?" she wanted to know next. "When you found 'er?"

"I brought her up to my bothy and took off her wet clothes,

and first I tried to let her lie on the settle, but she was so cold, so I wrapped her in the quilt and held her next to me, in front of the range."

"So was you 'olding 'er when she died?" Marigold wanted to know, and for the first time she turned her eyes away from the sea and looked directly at me.

"I was," I told her.

Marigold gave a sort of sigh and reached out to hold my hand.

"I's glad about that," she told me.

At that point, Malcolm came out with the tea. He gave me a questioning look, and I nodded. *Aja*, it would be good if he joined us.

"We've been talking about the night I found Lavender," I told him.

"That was a terrible night," Malcolm said. "Of course, that was before I arrived back on the island. But I've seen her grave."

"I 'aven't," Marigold told us.

I felt suddenly guilty. We had been so busy renovating the bothy, helping the newcomers, planting our fields and preparing for the short summer, and wee Lavender had been buried before we had known Marigold or the other refugees. How could we have forgotten to organise such an obvious thing, as showing Rose and Si's family where Lavender was buried?

I saw the frown on Malcolm's face, and I knew he was thinking the same thing.

"We'll take you," he said. "We should have taken you there sooner. She's buried over on Aeloff's Hill, in a beautiful cemetery overlooking the sea. It's where my grandfather is buried, my *pari-pari*."

"She might be frightened, so near to the sea…" Marigold looked worried.

"*Nei*." Malcolm was reassuring. "It's way up high, safe from the biggest waves. Like Marie's bothy, or mine. And lots of good *bondii* are buried there. They'll look after her."

I thought Marigold looked a little less sad. "And you'll take me there?" she checked. "And I can say goodbye?"

★★★

Si had taken to island life. He was as surprised about it as us. "I didn't never 'ave a proper job," he told Malcolm, "not before the sea came up. I worked in the supermarket ware'ouse but they made 'alf of us redundant when that recession 'appened and there weren't that much food to unload. I emptied bins for a bit, but I didn't like it, and the money weren't that good. And I couldn't do nothing else because of... well, you know, I couldn't read. Then the sea pretty much took over the town, and we was all moved out. They said it were just temporary, so when I was taken off to a different camp from the uvers I fought, well, we'll all be together again soon. I ain't never seen nor 'eard of 'em since. My aunt and cousins, and my aunt's boyfriend... for all I know, they's all dead – or maybe settled 'appily somewhere. 'O knows?"

Both he and Rose were carving niches for themselves in Gamla Hus. Sigrid had encouraged Rose to turn her hammock-making into a small business. Together they had ordered coloured cord from Aberdeen, but Sigrid wanted them to move to dying their own as soon as possible. Petter and Malchi had installed a hammock in the *fi'ilsted* and put coloured lights, driftwood and shells in it, to make a sort of feature and to light up the corner furthest from the fire. Sigrid had ordered hammocks to store sports equipment in the school, and Tom, down at the ferry port in Storhaven, had agreed to sell hammocks to the crews who manned the ferry. Malchi was going to take photos that could be used as advertising materials.

Si had planted his potatoes, having refined the process while working out at the St Matthew's Bay bothy. Now that the villagers were talking about floating their boats again down at the summer harbour, Si was keen to learn how to fish. Since there was very little land attached to their bothy, and most of that was now taken up with potato plants, the little family would need fish just to survive. Settlement grants wouldn't last forever. The *Oyrod* had never, at that time, been prepared to give food aid in lean times, and we *bondii* had never cared to challenge that decision.

It was at about this time, before the boats were actually launched, that the refugee called Harry arrived in Gamla Hus. He came over to work with Yanni Sinclair, moving the huge stones with which the new bothy would be built. He and Si were obviously quite good friends from their years out at the old airport, although there was quite an age difference. Harry was tall and thin, with greying hair and a naturally severe expression, although his eyes crinkled up when he smiled his slow smile. Harry and Si were recruited by Yanni to crew his rowing boat when the time came, and the two men sat companionably in the *fi'ilsted* some evenings, gleaning any information any of the regulars could give them about fish stocks and the general business of harvesting the sea.

Marigold, though, didn't want her father to go to sea. She stood with me one afternoon, looking down at the summer harbour. There was, I thought, an even closer bond between us since she had talked to me about the night her sister had died. The waves were rolling up the loch and breaking against the old sea wall. It must have been low tide, because even then that old solid rock construction was completely covered when the tide was high. One or two of the boat owners had started the labour of bringing down their fragile-looking rowing boats from the high, rocky ledge where they had been kept and worked on during the winter.

"The sea's so big!" Marigold commented. "It just goes on and on forever!"

"Well, in a way," I agreed. "Has Sigrid shown you any maps? It does more or less join up around the world."

The bairn was quiet. Then, "If my paps fell into the water," she suggested, "'e could be taken almost anywhere by them waves – to India or Iceland or even…" she was struggling to think of faraway places. "Even France!"

I rested my hand gently on the wee lassie's shoulder. I knew she was thinking again of the night that her little sister had been washed out to sea. How could she not recall what she had seen with her own eyes, or the futile attempts of the refugees to save her? Now that we had talked about it, now that the story was out in the open between us, it seemed as if Marigold referred to it more often in our conversation. She was, I thought, haunted by her memories of that night. Her fear of the waves was not unfounded, after all.

I tried to comfort her. "They don't take the boats out if the sea's rough. And the fishermen look out for each other, you know. There're usually two or three of those little boats quite close to each other – within shouting distance. And they all wear life jackets, to hold them up in the water if an accident happens."

"Lavender couldn't swim," the bairn told me. "My paps can. 'E learnt when 'e was a boy. 'E lived by the sea then, too, but the sea came up and took away their town."

"Yes," I agreed. "I heard about that. The sea has taken away a lot of towns, but it won't reach Gamla Hus, that's for sure!"

Marigold sighed and nestled up against me. "I likes it," she told me, "all this." She waved a hand in the general direction of the waves rolling up between the steep rocky slopes. "I likes the birds and the wind and them tiny little plants what grow flowers in the rocks. When we lived… when we was slaves, I used to lie by the fire next to Mum and you could 'ear the wind ripping at the broken roof and the big waves down on the beach and my dad snoring and Frankie talking in 'er sleep, and I was glad what I wasn't in no town, like where Mum grew up, 'aving to go to school and be 'it by other kids. I thinks En-Somi is better. But I wish Lavender 'adn't died."

What could I say? I wished it too. We watched Yanni and Robert lift Yanni's boat down the steep slope to the flatter land where, already, two other boats were resting upside down on the grass. For a few minutes neither of us said anything.

"I thinks about 'er all the time," Marigold was speaking quietly, almost to herself. "I thinks that if she were still alive, she would sleep on the bottom bunk wiv me. I thinks what we could go to school together and look after Thistle together. If Lavender were 'ere I would let 'er 'ave all my best things – my new jacket what you and Malcolm got for me and the stone with a bit of pink in it, what Andy gave me, and my book about where babies come from which Shona gave me, although we knew all that stuff already, me and Lavender!" Suddenly she grinned up at me. "We watched Quincy and Mo out on the sand dunes in the summer. Afterwards they was always 'appy! Almost always. And my mum and dad, by the fire at night…"

I laughed out loud. "Yes, it makes people happy," I agreed.

"Do you and Malcolm…?"

"Enough!" I commanded, still laughing. "That's not a question you should ask people!"

"I think you does!" asserted the bairn, mischievously.

CHAPTER 15

L yle was in difficulty.

Malcolm had suggested that I accompany him over to Storhaven, to look at the progress on the St Matthew's Bay bothy and to have a meal at the Castle *fi'ilsted*. We were to stay at Verity's for two or three nights.

It was a Friday, I remember. For a couple of weeks there had been no ferry – not the weather, this time, but industrial action or an engine problem, I can't recall so far back. Anyway, I do remember arriving in the little town pretty much at the same time as the *North Atlantic Seabird* docked. There was a lot of cargo, two or three weeks' worth of orders including some white goods for the bothies that were being rebuilt or renovated and three goats donated by some people in Shetland for those setting up as crofters for the first time. Alf Kullander was helping Tom and a crew member with startlingly wild red hair to unload bundles of copper piping for the new-build bothy they were planning just north of their place, on the lower slopes of Norse Hill. It was more or less agreed that Frankie, her son-in-law Eric and her granddaughter Shirley would live there, and there was some talk of moving that little family unit over to Gamla Hus now that the weather was easing up. They would live at the Kullanders' place until the bothy was ready for them, and Eric could help with the construction. It would be one less family for Verity to worry about.

Shawn and his father had come into town from the St Matthew's Bay bothy and were helping to lift heavy electrical goods off the ferry. Jeannie was down on the quay, probably intending to pick up something for the tea rooms but actually talking in an animated fashion to Sheena, who would eventually move in with Charlie. I didn't recognise Sheena, to be honest. Like all the *un-fedii*, incomers, she looked quite different now that she was dressed more like *En-Som-in-Fedii*, and she was not a refugee I had spoken to much over at the old airport. It was a happy, busy scene, being filmed, of course, by the Alba crew. I think that was the first time I saw Elise talking to Harris, our home-grown rebel.

Lyle was in uniform. He rarely wore his *nasyoni* garb over in Hus, but he was carrying a lot of responsibility now and was still young. I suppose he needed to assert his authority. While Malcolm was talking to a group of old friends from his schooldays, I watched Lyle. Two of the crew members came up to him, gesticulating angrily. I saw him stand patiently, listening, then answering. He took out his phone and, I imagine, made some notes, and the crewmen smiled and one of them shook his hand. Tom took a break from unloading the piping and said something over his shoulder to Lyle, then thumped him on the shoulder in a friendly fashion. Two *harkrav*, a man and a woman, approached him, looking angry. I saw Lyle shaking his head negatively as he answered their question, and they came away, frowning. Two of the Storhaven children went running up to him and said something, and I saw him laughing, but as soon as they skipped away, there was a frown on his face again.

On the other side of the quay, where the old ticket booth served as shelter for people waiting for the ferry, Verity was standing with Holti and Ingrid Fraser. They appeared to be deep in conversation. I saw Lyle look across at them, then look away, then look back again. I felt a sudden, deep sadness for Lyle. In all my thirty-something years I had never had a broken heart and now, partnered with Malcolm, I thought I never would. Lyle's wretchedness was written all over his face.

Verity was not much better off. Friday was a working day for her, so it was difficult to find time for much talk, but it was obvious that she had lost a lot of that carefree spirit which had made her such good company as we started to track down the villains only a few months earlier. We had hoped to take her to the Castle that evening, but she said that she had to go out to Caldbrae to talk to one of her congregation and would not be back until late.

We finally caught up with her over breakfast. She was already up when I emerged, sitting at her kitchen table with a mug of tea and her laptop open in front of her.

"*Morgoni*," she said, in a distracted sort of way, not looking up from the screen. "There's tea in the pot."

I poured two mugs full and took one through to Malcolm. He's not usually a man to sleep in – even less, in those days – but we had drunk more than usual the night before and gone to bed later than was our custom. It had seemed impolite to settle down for the night before Verity got back.

I sat at the kitchen table opposite the young minister. She was typing something, pausing, apparently checking it through, then she must have clicked on 'send'. She sat back and sighed.

"I'm writing to the moderator," she told me. "I need to sort out some things."

"Oh dear," was all I could think to say. "Will she be able to help?"

"I think so…" Verity was looking over my shoulder, out of the high kitchen window, where banks of grey cloud seemed to be lined up in an orderly fashion, creeping southwards. "She has a reputation for kindness, and her ministry started young, like mine. I think she'll be understanding."

I waited, hoping Verity would say more but not wanting to press her. I had never been one for organised religion and I didn't know what the moderator could say or do that Verity's friends here on the island couldn't contribute.

We could hear Malcolm pottering through to the bathroom, and the loo flushed. Outside, a sudden gust of wind blew a smattering of rain against the window.

"I think it might be best if I leave here," Verity told me at last. "It isn't fair on Lyle, me being around all the while. And perhaps the kirk needs a more experienced minister. I didn't realise, when I said I wanted to come here…"

"But I think the islanders love you!" I exclaimed. "Would God really want you to go away from a place where you are doing so much good, and leave a man who is so devoted to you? Could any god wish that?"

She sighed. "You make it sound so straightforward," she told me. "But it isn't. Well, I don't think it is. When I was ordained, it was to serve here, in this kirk. If I can't serve properly, if I'm torn two ways… there was a prayer in my ordination service, where we asked that we would seek God's kingdom before anything else. How can I put God first if I'm in a relationship with someone who isn't even a believer? Oh, Marie, I'm not sure I should ever have come here!"

I'll admit that it sounded crazy to me. "But lots of ministers are married!" I pointed out. "In Melrose there was a guy who had five bairns! I mean, he wasn't exactly celibate!"

Verity chuckled at that. "It's not to do with celibacy!" she corrected me. "It's to do with priorities and loyalties. There's a phrase in the Bible, that you can't serve God and mammon. If you marry someone who shares your priorities, that's one thing, but Lyle… and yet he's such a good man!"

Malcolm came into the room at that point. He must have heard Verity's last explanation. He took his mug over to the counter, checked the teapot (which was empty) and filled the kettle again. Then he sat at the table.

"Are you sure that 'serving God' is the same as 'agreeing to the same creed'? I mean, don't you think you were both serving God when we were hunting down those villains? Don't you and Lyle share the same values?"

"Oh, Malcolm!" Verity sounded frustrated. "Don't you think I've considered that? But then there's the other thing, the business of staying on the island. What if I felt called to serve somewhere else? Lyle doesn't want to leave En-Somi. His family is here, he wants to bring up his children here... I couldn't ask it of him!"

I looked across at Malcolm. He had a serious expression, a slight frown on his face. I felt a surge of love for him.

"Marie and I..." he began. Then he looked at me and smiled. "We're praying for you. For both of you. Holding you in the Light."

Verity looked momentarily taken aback. "You are?" she exclaimed. Then, more quietly, "Thank you."

Malcolm winked at me.

★★★

It was, I suppose, only a couple of days later that Frankie, Eric and young Shirley arrived outside the *fi'ilsted* in Hus, in a cart pulled by only one sturdy little pony, and followed by the Alba crew on a second cart. They had been sleeping in the kirk and had very few belongings, although little Shirley was clutching a very lifelike baby doll dressed in a Babygro and a woolly hat.

Fiona Kullander had walked down the hill to meet them, and Andy had come along too. I was there at Fiona's request, because she felt that it was important that someone the *un-fedii* knew was there to ease the process. The refugees had met the Kullanders briefly before, over in Storhaven, but they hadn't been across the island to the village. They stood in the street looking around them, apparently not sure what to make of it all. I suppose the village looks very primitive if you've started to become used to the cobbled streets and sturdy buildings of the town.

"*Hei!*" Fiona greeted her new house guests. "Did you have a good ride over? I bet it was wet up on top!"

"Yeah, soaking," agreed Frankie.

Eric was looking around at our small huddle of bothies, at the shop with its turf roof and the track, which that morning had a small stream trickling down its centre. "Quiet sort of place!" he commented.

I laughed. "We have our moments! What's the plan, Fiona? Are we going straight up to your place?"

"I think so, if that suits you?" She was talking to her visitors. "I thought you might like to see your rooms and have something hot for lunch after that trip over Fyrtarn Fjell pass? It's quicker if we walk from here. Are you up for that?"

"Oh, yeah!" It was Frankie again. "We's as strong as oxes! And Eric can carry the kid if 'e needs to." She glanced at the *fi'ilsted* and added, "So you've got yer own pub? Can't be all bad over 'ere, then!"

"It's all good!" exclaimed Andy. "Do you want to hold my hand on the way up?" He was talking to wee Shirley. "It can be quite steep. I'm Andy. What's your name?"

The bairn sidled more closely against the long, dark coat which Frankie continued to wear, left over from the old airport days. She didn't answer Andy.

"The wee lassie is shy," Fiona told her son. "Give her time to get her bearings. Come on, it's this way. Mind that rock!"

★★★

I stayed for lunch and saw the three refugees settled into their rooms. The Kullanders' place is unique on En-Somi, built with oil money back before oil was a dirty word, and in the style of a Norwegian farmhouse. It is large – the Kullanders had raised their brood there, and I think Alf's mam had lived in the room on the side after his paps had died. Alf and Fiona had given Eric a room in the attic and put Frankie and wee Shirley in the two girls' rooms over the kitchen. I learnt from Fiona a day or two later, though, that the bairn wouldn't sleep in a room on her own.

"It's not surprising, when you think about it," Fiona commented. "I gather they all slept together round their fire in the old airport. And since then, they've been sleeping in the kirk. That wee one has always had people around her. We've moved her bed into Frankie's room. It seems to be working out."

"And how is it for you?" I wanted to know.

"Well… interesting!" was all Fiona would tell me. "And educational!"

★★★

It was as I was walking back down to Hus, the day that Frankie and her family arrived, that I bumped into Elise. She was standing outside the shop, staring in the direction of Malcolm's bothy, although you can't actually see it from there, only the top of his wind turbine which was whirling wildly in the northeaster that was making late April feel like November.

"Hi, Marie!" She looked pleased to see me. "Have they settled in, the refugees?"

"It's early days," I answered. "They're going through so many changes. It was a bit of a culture shock when I arrived here – I can't imagine what they're making of it all!"

We were standing side by side, looking westwards. You can't see the sea from the village, but we could hear it in the distance. Seabirds were reeling overhead, squawking and screeching. Closer by, sheep on the moors were cropping the spring grass as if it were a calm, summer's day. From their pen behind the shop, Shona's goats were bleating.

"So, what do you think of the decision of the *Oyrod*?" Elise wanted to know.

I didn't know they had made any significant decisions. "About what?" I wanted to know.

"I thought you might not have heard." Elise was frowning, though whether it was from the wind in her face, or the news she was about to give me, I couldn't tell. "About the changes to your island taxes," she explained. "They had a meeting last night. *In camera* according to Ingrid. They've voted to increase the land taxes and freeze the taxation on incomes and investments. So the costs incurred by having the refugees here will fall on the *bondii* who farm the land, and not on the *harkrav*."

I was stunned. For a moment I didn't say anything. Then, "I need to find Malcolm," I told her. "This'll hit some of us really hard."

"That's what I thought," agreed the young reporter. "Island life seems to have far more intrigue attached to it than I ever thought when I first started to learn about En-Somi!"

CHAPTER 16

Perhaps if we hadn't all been so concerned about this sleight of hand of the *Oyrod*, we might have paid closer attention to what was going on among the bairns. But as it was, the news Elise had given me was doing the rounds of the island all that day. As soon as one or two heard what the council had decided, phones were buzzing and pinging all across En-Somi. Malcolm texted that he'd see me in the *fi'ilsted*, and it seemed many other people had the same idea. By 3pm when school was out, a crowd had gathered; Petter and Malchi were doing a roaring trade with the drink, although it was the wrong time of day for eating.

"How can they get away with it?" Jamie MacLoughlan wanted to know. "Half my land is unproductive. With the land reforms we were granted the cliffs all the way round to Michaelmas Fjell, but you can't grow anything there! We just collect a few eggs in the spring…"

"I'm raising a family from sheep and fishing," Yanni added. "The price of lamb dipped to an all-time low last autumn, and we can't export our herring or whiting by law, only the mackerel. I'll be feeding my bairns on potatoes and neeps! It'll be like the Irish famine!"

"And there's those *harkrav* with money in the bank and shares in companies in Edinburgh and Oslo! They wouldn't even notice an extra five per cent on their incomes! But five per cent on our land values…" Shona was furious, almost choking on her words.

Petter was standing behind the bar, with a mug of tea in his hand. "I spoke to Ingrid Fraser on the phone," he said. "She and Holti tried to persuade the rest of the *Oyrod* of the consequences of such a move, but, you know, they're in the minority."

Sigrid was frowning into her tankard of beer. "Of course," she told us, "it's partly our fault. We've always elected a majority of *harkrav* onto the *Oyrod*."

"*Aja*! But they're still there to represent us!" Shona's face was bright red with indignation.

"Perhaps we are too traditional, after all," Malcolm suggested. "I know that my mam and paps always voted for Fox-Drummin's father when I was a wee bairn. He seemed to know what he was doing, and he had useful connections…"

"*Aja*." Patrick had just come in, and had heard the last comment. "It's as if we believed they had the right to govern us – as if we swallowed the idea that the *harkrav* are better at that sort of thing."

Elise was looking from side to side, taking in everything that was being said.

"So, when are the next elections?" she wanted to know. "When can you vote them out?"

Malcolm laughed out loud. "Oh, Elise!" he exclaimed. "I think you should come and live here!"

"Not for another two years," I explained.

"I'll be bankrupt by then!" Yanni had turned from being angry to despondent. "We'll have to leave En-Somi!"

"And there's another problem…" Robert was thinking aloud. "We won't have any cash. I mean, actual money. Like, in our bank accounts. I can't be alone – the only currency I see comes from hiring out my ponies and cart, and I use every last penny of it on stuff I can't grow or make – things I buy in your shop, Shona, or over the internet. But taxes have to be paid in pounds and pence – we can't pay them in neeps and potatoes! Every last penny'll have to go on the increased taxes. How will we buy essentials: wood or slate from the mainland, or paint, or things you women need? You'll lose all your trade in the shop, Shona and Patrick."

There was a depressed silence as we all considered the truth of this.

It was at that point that Olaf entered the *fi'ilsted*. He looked old and bowed down – and happy.

Looking around, seeing our miserable expressions and noticing, of course, the quiet in the room, he asked, "So why the long faces? Has the summer solstice been cancelled?"

Everyone started to talk at once, trying to explain the news to Olaf. He stood, patiently, listening to one gloom-ridden tale after another. He heard us all out, taking a tankard from Petter and looking thoughtful.

Then, "*Aja*, I heard all about that this morning," he told us.

"It's a catastrophe!" Jamie told him. "Don't you realise?"

"Well, *nei*." Olaf took a gulp of his beer and wiped the froth from his lips with the back of his hand. "It will be no catastrophe! Not unless we *En-Som-in-Fedii* have lost our backbone! It'll be a struggle, no doubt. And we'll need to stick together and help each other out. But have we nae done that before? Remember when *Mori-mori* Cadha's roof blew off? Or when old Buck Stewart lost his ponies?"

"This is a bit more serious than that!" Worry was making Yanni sound sulky.

"*Aja*, a bigger challenge," Olaf agreed. "And it'll be a bigger triumph in the end!"

In the soft lighting of the *fi'ilsted*, faces looked unimpressed.

"How can we fight it?" Jamie wanted to know. "They're the *Oyrod*. They make the rules."

I had the beginnings of an idea. "If I tell Bjorn what's happening," I suggested slowly, thinking aloud, "I bet he'd make us a loan to help pay the taxes, just for two years... until we can vote for a different *Oyrod*."

"And I have a pension," added Malcolm. "Actual cash. And not much land to pay taxes on…"

"Yanni, won't your brother help you?" Patrick was looking more optimistic. "He's working on the ferries. They pay good money."

"We could start a communal fund," Petter suggested. "Keep a record of who contributes what, and make sure everyone is paid back, when all this is over."

"My daughter would keep the books," Sigrid offered. "She's a whizz with money and accounting!"

"And actually," Jamie had cheered up a bit too, "a person can live quite well on potatoes, kale and lamb!"

"And fish!" Malchi reminded everyone.

Olaf turned to Elise. "Now, young lassie," he said, pronouncing 'young' like the dialect word, *ung*, "we'll need you to keep a record of all this – film us, interview us, tell the story. You do it on the film, and I'll do it in the song." He grinned around the room. "And we'll see those refugees settled among us, just as we planned! After all, that's what this is all about, isn't it?"

★★★

Shirley, it seemed, had been keen to start school. Andy Kullander was right there, in the same house as the bairn, filling her head with stories of all the exciting things that happened in Sigrid's classroom. And she had less to be anxious about. At just six years old she wouldn't be far behind her peers, nor was she old enough to worry about such things. Frankie, too, wanted her granddaughter to play with other children. "It were the best bit about school when I were a kid," she told Fiona. "Sports and crafts and playing in the playground. Mind you, that were years ago and in Portsmouth! A bit different from up 'ere!"

They had to invent a birthday for the child, to register her.

"'Er muvver would 'ave known," Frankie said. "I remembers it were in the spring. But 'er mum ain't 'ere no more…"

"Well then, let's say 10th May," suggested Sigrid. "That way she can have a party at school." We were all getting quite good at inventing biographical details for the refugees by then.

What we didn't reckon on was the effect Shirley's presence might have on Marigold.

★★★

Most of the *bondii* across the island shared the indignation of those of us in the west, when it came to the increased taxation. Apart from a few families in the town, we were all people of the land, land that was rocky and badly drained, land that could barely support us, but on which we would now have to pay more tax. And those payments would demand cash, actual money, and a lot of families went weeks without using money at all. We milked our cows and goats, cared for our chickens; we grew our kale and oats and a little barley over on the south of the island. We ate fish from our own waters, lamb from our own grazing and potatoes from our own ground. It was true that in Storhaven there were folk who were employed, who had contracts and wages paid into bank accounts, but they were few and far between: Kirsty who ran the bank and also the Storhaven branch of the post office; a nurse; Tom who worked at the ferry port; Verity, the minister of the kirk; the *nasyonii;* and probably one or two others. Jeannie, of course, handled actual money at her café, and the school-teachers were paid small salaries, but all-in-all, the amount of cash that circulated on the island or ended up in bank accounts didn't amount to much.

We did a lot of deals that didn't involve money. Actually, we still do. I no longer supply the *fi'ilsted* with driftwood in exchange for fish as I did in those days, I'm too old to drag the old sledge up to the village, but there are others who do, and who provide me with salad in the summer in payment for the use of my beach. Back then I earned a little actual money from selling the *gensii* I knitted at the ferry port, but more often than not, if I had a commission from a fellow islander, I was paid in kind: dressed crab, or goats' cheese maybe, whisky from someone's still or repairs done to my dry-stone walls.

★★★

"It's pretty vindictive." Malcolm was thinking aloud. We were in his bothy, and I was stirring the stew while he stood at one of his tall, narrow windows looking out on the muckle scarf stacks which would soon turn white, in places, from the bird droppings. It was evening but before sunset – our evenings are long by May. "The *harkrav* must know how hard some of the islanders are going to find all this!"

"I'm not sure they do," I answered. "I reckon there's some of them who've never been inside one of our homes. Their kids don't go to school with ours; the parents don't work with us. Sometimes I feel as if we're one big film set, as if we're just a backdrop to their very different lives."

Malcolm turned and looked at me. "But they can't all be like that, can they?"

I took two bowls down from the rack above the hob, where they had been warming, and started to ladle out the stew. "*Nei*," I agreed. "At least, I dare say some of them wish us well – or, at least, they don't wish us any harm. I think they just don't know how different the world looks if you're living on Norse Hill or out on Caldbrae."

He came to the table, poured us each a glass of water and spooned mashed potato on top of his stew. "Mm!" Malcolm was always appreciative of his food!

"But this," he added, after a mouthful or two, "this land taxation scheme – it has to be a deliberate plan."

"*Aja.*" I thought about it for a moment. "It almost feels like revenge," I added. "They wanted the refugees off the island, and we defied them. Now they're making us pay."

Malcolm grinned. "It isn't going to work, is it? Yanni has redoubled his efforts to cart the last of the stone up from the old bothy to its new location, and Alf plans to enrol Eric's help to start on the foundations of their new bothy. It's going to be a busy summer."

"Oh, and Bjorn has paid quite a contribution into our communal land tax fund. And the kids in Lerwick are doing a fundraiser…"

Malcolm chuckled. "Olaf was right, you know," he said. "We're going to win this one!"

★★★

Wee Shirley made an immediate hit in the village school. Whereas Marigold did everything she could to fit in, dressing like the other bairns and gradually adopting their ways of speaking, Shirley stood out. Frankie had cut her hair short, and it framed her face in blonde curls. Once their first order of new clothes arrived, she was the only child in the school to wear a dress and tights instead of trousers. She looked like a little doll, and many of the island children treated her as such.

And Shirley was a chatterbox. She told the other bairns about her life over at the old airport and about sleeping in the kirk. It seems she quickly realised that the more dramatic her stories, the more attention the other children paid her. Perhaps she was a little spoiled in a way, by her grandmother Frankie and her uncle Eric, but if she was, I cannot feel it within me to blame anyone. We learnt later that she held court during breaks from lessons, describing the horrors of life over in St Matthew's Bay, the villainous 'bosses' and the terrible food. In Shirley's world everyone was either very good or very bad. The refugees were very good. Verity, who let them sleep in her kirk, was also positively saintly. The 'bosses', of course, were extremely bad. I suppose her view of the world was typical of many small children – and not a few adults. Sigrid was aware that Marigold never contributed to these stories, that she would walk away, sometimes retreating back into the classroom to draw a picture or to look at a book. She was aware, too, that young Christian hung on every word Shirley uttered, horror written all over his face, like a bairn listening to ghost stories in the dark.

Maybe, if we had all been a little more alert, no harm would have come of all the bairn's chatter. Sooner or later, the other children would have tired of wee Shirley's stories. Sigrid was keeping her eye on the situation and saw no reason for concern. Sometimes, she told me later, you just have to let children work things out of their systems.

Then, on the day of her birthday party, Shirley's chatter reverberated onto Marigold, and none of us saw it coming.

Of course, I didn't know the whole story until much later. Sigrid always marked the birthdays of her pupils, and it was not unusual for parties to take place in the school before the bairns dispersed to their bothies anywhere within a five-mile radius. Usually, one or other parent would stop by after lessons to help to organise games and to deliver the regulation birthday cake. Both Frankie and Eric turned up at the school on the 10th, as planned, with a feast provided by Fiona, who had explained the customs.

All went exactly as expected. Frankie brought the cake in, candles alight, and a beaming Shirley blew them out and made her wish. A game of pass-the-parcel saw Elin winning a much-coveted torch that would shine yellow or red, and musical statues resulted in a play-off between the twins. When the cake was cut all the bairns were told to sit down as slices were distributed by Frankie and Sigrid.

And that's when things went wrong.

"Is that your mam?" asked one of the other five-year-olds.

"Nah!" Shirley was mildly contemptuous. "That's my granny."

"So, where's your mam?"

Nobody can blame Shirley for the way she handled that question. She didn't want to talk about her mother. Maybe she just didn't have an answer. She was just a little thing, and she instinctively deflected the question.

"Ain't got one!" she said. "Us refugees, we 'ave lots of dead people in our families! We's been slaves, and slaves is treated really cruelly. I ain't got no mum, like Marigold ain't got no sister! That girl what drowned on Marie's beach, that were 'er sister!"

Suddenly all eyes turned on Marigold.

"I 'as got a sister!" Marigold objected. "You seen 'er. Baby Thistle! You leave Lavender out of this, Shirley!"

But it was too late. Christian, eyes wide, was staring at Marigold. And of course, the business of Lavender being found on my beach had worried Christian so much that his parents had sheltered him from the tale. They had carefully never discussed the matter in front of him. "Was that your sister?" he asked, almost breathless. "The bairn on the beach? The one who died?" He might have been the only child in the room who didn't already know it – and easily the most fascinated by the story.

Young Elin butted in. Like many of the bairns, she had heard all about it at home. "Of course it was!" she announced, going over to Marigold and holding her hand. "Everyone knows that. But if Marigold doesn't want to talk about it…"

But wee Shirley was too young, or was enjoying being the centre of attention too much, to take the hint.

"She were washed away by a big wave!" the bairn announced, holding her hand up in the air to demonstrate how high the water had been. "It were bigger than my uncle Eric, bigger than…" she paused, trying, I suppose, to think of something huge, to make the comparison. "Bigger than a mountain! And it washed

145

Lavender away into the sea, and she weren't never seen again! And the fishes ate 'er!"

Marigold burst into tears. "Why did you 'ave to say that?" she sobbed, looking at Shirley. "I's trying not to think about 'er. I's pretending what it never 'appened. And now you gone and spoiled it all!" And she tore her hand from Elin's and ran out of the school room.

Then Shirley, being only a wee one herself and not sure what she had done wrong, also burst into tears. Christian was turning from one person to another, wanting to know more – or to be told that none of it was true. All the bairns seemed to be talking at once. By the time the general hubbub had calmed down and peace restored, it was time for the party to end. Bairns donned their outdoor gear and shifted their backpacks onto their backs, ready for their walks home. Nobody wondered about Marigold. She lived just up the track, beyond the shop. She was probably home, telling her mam what had happened or playing with her baby sister. Nobody thought to check.

CHAPTER 17

At the time, of course, I knew none of this. Malcolm was over at St Matthew's Bay again, putting in the insulation and helping with the plumbing. I had been tending my vegetable plot, not needing to wear my thick jacket for the first time that year and feeling optimistic about the approaching summer. Duncan was coming home for the May break; the weather forecast was good; and when Bjorn and I had talked over Skype about the loan, he had mentioned how much Duncan liked Malcolm.

It's easy to work late into the evening in May. The sun doesn't set until 8.30pm or so, and I find that if I'm engrossed in something, the time just passes. It was only when I realised how long the shadows had grown that I started thinking about eating.

I had left my phone on the kitchen counter. I took off my gardening clogs and gloves and dropped them into the chest under the coat hooks. I hung up my jacket and washed my hands, then put the kettle on. Finally, not expecting anything except perhaps a message from Malcolm, I checked my phone.

I had three missed calls from Sigrid. I clicked on the app to hear the message, half expecting it to be something about the knitting co-operative. We were still thinking of starting classes for the refugees.

"*Hei*, Marie!" I thought she sounded a little tense. "Sorry to bother you. I'm guessing you've got Marigold with you. Can you phone back and let me know? There was a bit of a problem at school today – she's probably told you all about it? Anyway, she didn't go home, and Rose is worried. Call me back when you pick this up, will you?"

I could almost feel the happiness drain out of me. I had a terrible sense of foreboding. My hand was shaking as I tapped 'reply' and waited for Sigrid's phone to ring.

As soon as she picked up, I blurted out, "Sigrid, she isn't here. Marigold, I mean. What happened?"

"Oh *nei!*" Sigrid sounded distressed. "I was sure she'd have come to you. The subject of Lavender came up. She's never mentioned her sister at school, but Shirley… anyhow, Marigold left the party early but she didn't go home."

"So where is she?" I asked, feeling panic rising inside me. "Will she have gone to Andy Kullander?"

"No, not there," Sigrid said. "We've already checked, and anyhow, that's where Shirley is…"

"And she isn't at Shona's, or confiding in Robert's ponies?"

"We've tried everyone," Sigrid told me. "Malcolm isn't answering his phone. Would she have gone there?"

"He's over in St Matthew's Bay," I answered. "There's sometimes a bad connection on that part of the island. She might have gone to his bothy. I'll go over there now, shall I, and check?"

"Would you?" Sigrid sounded slightly relieved. "It'll be getting dark soon, and that wee lassie doesn't know her way around yet, not well. Keep in touch, will you?"

The sun was hovering right on the horizon as I left the bothy. The sheep were still baaing; the gulls were still crying; the wind was light and gentle, but the day had lost its charm completely.

I called as I strode across the moor to the burn. "Marigold! Marigold! It's me, Marie. Marigold! Marigold!"

There was no answer.

★★★

By the time I had reached Malcolm's bothy and found it deserted, Sigrid had contacted Lyle, and Lyle had reached Si, intercepting him on his way home to Hus. Almost the whole island was alerted – certainly everyone on our side of En-Somi and in Storhaven. The long dusk was fading into darkness; I could see torch lights flickering on the moors above Gamla Hus as I walked up to the village; and I could hear voices: "Marigold! Marigold!"

Rose was standing at the door of Bothan Ros, a soft glow behind her and Thistle on her hip. She looked awful, like a wax-work model of a person, badly executed. There was a sort of stiffness about her, and when I tried to give her a hug, it was like embracing a standing stone.

"I knew it were too good to last," she said, in a cool, distant sort of voice. "There weren't no way me and Si was going to live 'appy ever after."

"Oh, Rose! We'll find her! We will! She can't have gone that far!" But my words sounded hollow.

"No," agreed Rose, still in that flat, dead voice. "She can't 'ave gone that far... down a cliff maybe, or drownded in a bog... per'aps fallen into the sea like 'er sister... and she ain't 'ad nofing to eat. She never came 'ome."

I felt helpless. The bairn was obviously not in any of the bothies on our side of the island. Most people were already out looking. "Would she go to her paps – her dad?" I wondered, "over towards St Matthew's Bay?"

"'E's on 'is way 'ere," she answered. "She ain't wiv 'im. Ain't nowhere. I fink we's lost 'er."

"But where else could she go? Who does she know?"

"She don't know nobody!" Rose's monotone voice sounded slightly indignant. "You knows that. We never slept in that church, like the uvers, we came straight over 'ere. She knows your Duncan and that Alana, and Andy, but 'e ain't seen 'er, and the kids in the school, but she ain't never been to their 'ouses, and if they knew where she was, they'd tell us... he's just gone.

I only 'as Thistle left. What'll 'appen to 'er? Somefing bad, you can be sure of that!"

Goodness, I wished Malcolm was there! I felt completely helpless.

Sigrid came up from the direction of the school. "Everyone's out looking," she told Rose. "Come on, let's go inside. That wee one is getting cold. Let's make some tea. I've got my phone here. We'll know as soon as they find her." She turned to me. "We've got people searching our side of Fyrtarn Fjell," she said, "and the Storhaven people are working out from the town. Would you be up to walking the pass, just in case…?"

"Of course." I think I was relieved to be given something to do. But surely, Marigold wouldn't venture up there on her own? Maybe, if she wanted to find her paps or… suddenly I had an idea.

"Sigrid!" I called, just as she was closing Rose's door. "Sigrid, does Marigold know Verity?"

"Of course she do!" It was Rose answering, sounding scornful. "She came to the airport. Our lot rescued 'er! Remember?"

"So would she go there, to Verity?" I wanted to know.

"She don't know where the vicar lives," Rose pointed out. "No more'n I do. 'Ow could she go there?"

"I thought of that," Sigrid answered. "Verity's phone's turned off. But she must know Marigold is missing. Everyone knows." Then, to Rose, "Come on, let's make that tea."

***

Bothan Ros, Si and Rose's cottage, was the last bothy in the village back then, if you were heading up the path going east. The track is pretty much uphill all the way to the pass, but it's easy-going at first. It was full night, but clear, and my night vision was good in those days. I had my torch with me, but I seem to remember that I didn't need it. Of course, I knew the path well; I had walked it countless times.

I called as I went, "Marigold! Marigold!" But I listened too. If the child was in trouble, if she were hurt, her cries might not be strong. I heard other voices coming across the cooling air, also calling for the bairn, and I saw odd flashes of torchlight as people searched the moors.

As I climbed towards the pass I started to notice, perhaps for the first time, places beside the track where the ground fell away steeply. At one point I thought I heard a noise, a moaning in the reeds a hundred feet or so below the track. "Marigold! Marigold, it's all right! I'm here!" I called as I slithered down the boggy slope towards the sound. But when I got there, it was just a sheep sheltering against a jutting rock. I called again, but there was no child there.

Up on top of the pass the island spread out before me; I paused to gather my breath and to think. Where did I go when I was Marigold's age, and upset? My ninth year had been tough for me. I had moved in with Granny by then, but I was missing my parents, my old school, the whole life that tragedy had forced me to leave behind. Granny had been so understanding. She was my father's mother, my only surviving grandparent. My family had never lived in Melrose but my parents were buried there because that was where Granny lived. We used to go to the cemetery every Tuesday after school to put fresh flowers on the grave. If I wanted to, though, I could walk down Huntley Road on my own; I didn't need to cross any busy roads, and I would just sit on the grass and think about my parents.

And then it occurred to me. Of course, Marigold might go to the cemetery, to Aeloff's Hill, where Lavender had been buried in an unmarked grave because at the time no one had known who she was.

I pulled my phone out of my pocket and found Lyle's number. It was engaged. I tried Malcolm. The call went straight to his answering service. I tried Verity, but her phone was switched off. Well, the best thing I could do was to keep walking towards

Storhaven and keep searching – and try phoning again in a few minutes.

Once I was over the pass and the track was more sheltered, I started to get hot. It wasn't a warm night, but I suppose I was striding along, fuelled by worry. I still couldn't get anyone on the west of the island to answer my calls. I texted Sigrid to ask if there was any news but only received the one, bleak word, *nei*, in response. I left the usual track to check the ruined chapel in the dip beyond the footpath that takes you to Stone Beach, but there were only sheep there and something that scuttled away – not a rat, there were none on the island then, as now. Probably it was a mouse. Not a child, at any rate. I called, but of course there was no reply, so I backtracked to the main path and kept going.

It was midnight when I finally got through to Malcolm. The line was poor, fading in and out.

"Where are you?" I asked.

At the same time, he said, "Have you found her?"

"*Nei.*" The conversation was difficult. There seemed to be a time-lag on the call, so that we spoke over each other, and there was some sort of whistling interference.

"I'm up by Holti's," Malcolm explained. "Over Caldbrae. We're combing the moors down towards the sea… where are you?"

"I'm walking towards Storhaven," I told him. "I've had an idea…"

"So you haven't found her?" Malcolm's voice was hard to decipher. "Marie, are you still there?"

"We haven't found her," I repeated. "I think she might be…"

"Marie? Marie? Are you there?" Malcolm sounded frantic. Then I heard him say, presumably to someone close by, "I've lost her. The phone's gone dead. I think they're still looking." Then the line cut out completely. When I tried to phone back, nothing at all happened.

There were a few lights in windows in Storhaven. I went straight to Verity's flat. The door at the foot of the stairs in her building was closed and firmly locked. There were no lights in her windows. I banged urgently on the door, hurting my knuckles, but there was no response.

I stood in the street, wondering what to do now. I really needed some coffee. I had come ridiculously ill-prepared. Should I go straight on to Aeloff's Hill or try to find someone to go with me? I tried Verity's number again. Her phone was still switched off. The cemetery is quite remote, out to the south-east looking over the sea. I was wary about heading out there without telling somebody where I was going.

"Marie!"

I whirled around. I had been peering at my phone and Lyle had come up behind me.

"Lyle!" I was relieved to see him. "Have they found Marigold?"

"*Nei.*" Lyle sounded troubled. "Half the town is out looking, but there's not a sign of her. And I don't think she would have made it this far. Do you?"

"*Aja*," I told him. "Actually, I think she might have done. I think she might have gone to the cemetery."

"But why…? Oh, of course! Lavender's grave. But it's a hell of a way for a wee bairn to walk, and does she even know the way?"

"She might," I told him. "She's always asking questions. Who knows what somebody might have told her? One of the children at school, maybe? Or someone over in Hus?"

"We should check," agreed Lyle. "Tom, down at the quay, is coordinating everything on this side of the island. He's got the best reception. There're people combing the moors, but it's hard to make contact with some of them. The signal for our phones isn't very good tonight. We don't think she'll have headed for Frigg Moor, but Mac MacLoughlan is keeping an eye open, and Fenna is out with their dogs." He sounded very organised. It was a relief, really, to be able to share my feeling of urgency.

"Have you walked over from Hus?" Lyle asked, as if he had just realised that it was unusual for me to be standing in a Storhaven street in the early hours of the morning.

"I checked the track over the pass," I explained. "We've got the western moors covered, as much as we can. And now I'm here, I thought I'd call on Verity," I added. "The bairn knows her."

"She's gone," answered Lyle, sounding bleak.

"What do you mean, gone?"

"She's left the island. Verity has. She must have left on Friday's ferry. I went to see her. I was going to say that we couldn't go on like this, avoiding each other. I wanted to tell her that we could just be friends, that I understood that her calling to the kirk came first. I was going to reassure her that I wouldn't put her under any pressure. But when I went to her flat, she had gone. Just locked everything up and left."

"Oh, *nei!*" I was devastated, sad for Lyle but sad for myself too – sad for the island.

"I talked to Ingrid. I thought that she and Verity were close, but she didn't know much. Just that she was to take Sunday's service, as she did before Verity came, and that everyone contributing to the food programme was to take everything directly to Holti in the kirk, not to Verity's flat. And I talked to Tom at the ferry terminal. He didn't remember Verity boarding the ferry, but it was madly busy on Friday because they were unloading so much stuff for the new bothies, to say nothing of a disputed order of the wrong sort of caulking for the boat they're building for Charlie and the others…"

I didn't know what to say. Lyle looked utterly wretched, as if he were in physical pain. I touched his arm gently, letting him know that I understood – that I sympathised.

"Well!" Lyle was pulling himself together. "If we're going to head south, you ought to have a rest and something to eat and drink. Jean's keeping the Copper Kettle open for volunteers. We'll all be useless if we don't look after ourselves!"

CHAPTER 18

Jean was alone in the café, sitting at one of the tables, her head in her hands. She looked up as we came in and gave us a weak smile.

"Coffee?" she offered. "Hot chocolate? Tea?" Then she must have noticed Lyle's face. "Whisky?"

"*Nei!*" Lyle smiled gratefully. "We've still got work ahead of us. We need clear heads."

"That poor child!" Jean said, not waiting for us to tell her what we wanted, pouring coffee, taking cheese sandwiches from under a glass cover and putting them on the table in front of us and joining us at our table. "She weren't even born when I left them, you know – when I came 'ere. It breaks yer 'eart, doesn't it?"

"We might find her," I suggested, "alive and well." I hated to hear Jean talk as if Marigold were already dead.

"*Aja*, you might," agreed Jean. "Sorry. I should be out there, helping…"

"*Nei, nei!*" Lyle was insistent. "Stay here! You're helping well enough. We can't all be out on the moors."

It was only when we left, ten minutes later, that I began to wish I had swapped my light summer jacket for something warmer before I had left home. But how was I to know? We walked through the town streets side-by-side, saying nothing, then turned south along the only metalled road on En-Somi. There was a breeze coming in off the sea, and I buttoned my jacket. Lyle glanced at me.

"Dressing for the climate, I see?" he commented, wryly.

"Huh! I was in my garden when Sigrid phoned," I explained. "I didn't think…"

Lyle patted me on the shoulder. "You won't come to any harm," he pointed out, "as long as we keep moving."

★★★

It might sound strange to you given that I live on such a small island, but I had rarely been out of Storhaven in this direction until about six months earlier. However, by the night I'm telling you about now, the road was quite familiar. Up to our left, on Floirean's Cnoc, there were no lights. Did the *harkrav* who lived in those luxurious, elegant bothies even know that a child was missing? Would they care? To our right we saw glimpses of sea, waves breaking lazily on rocks or sand, white surf in the darkness. The hill where the cemetery had been established at some point unknown years ago, loomed up ahead. When had I last been there? Probably for *Mori-mori* Cadha's burial, before I had even met Malcolm, before I had known that there were refugees on the island.

We passed the steep, rocky, western side of the hill and then turned onto the track that takes you to the graveyard. It's a cobbled path now, but back then it was just rock and earth with grass growing down the middle. We walked in single file, although it was possible, even then, for a cart carrying a coffin to be driven up to the cemetery. All the graves are on the flatter top of the hill so that a visitor bringing flowers can stand and stare out to sea. It's moorland up there – peat bogs, I'm told. It may be that the bodies of those we have loved and lost will be preserved for eternity, like the bog bodies found in Denmark, but such things weren't on my mind that night.

I hadn't visited Lavender's grave, but Lyle had been there at the burial – it was the first time he had seen Verity, although they hadn't spoken to each other then. He led the way, past lichen-covered stone markers and a Celtic cross standing at a strange angle, to a small mound in the shelter of a dry-stone wall.

There was no sign of Marigold.

We stood in the darkness and listened to the sounds of the sea, of reeds beyond the wall, rustling in the breeze. One lonely gull cried out and was silent again. On the moor beyond the cemetery, sheep stirred. There were no other signs of life.

"Well, she's not here!" remarked Lyle, speaking softly as if we were in a kirk.

"*Nei…*" I was thinking about when I used to visit my parents' graves, how I would bring them flowers when Granny bought them for me, or small gifts of my own: things I had made at school, even a Christmas card once, although it went soggy and the felt-tip colours ran. I knelt down by the small mound, feeling sad.

"Oh, Lyle, look!" From close to the ground, I could see what hadn't been obvious when I was standing – stones carefully arranged in the shape of an L, and other stones making a heart shape.

Lyle squatted beside me. "Well," he said slowly, "so she has been here, anyhow… or somebody has."

I stood again. "But where would she go now?" I wondered.

Lyle also stood again, shrugging his jacket more comfortably onto his shoulders, staring around in the darkness.

"She might not be too far away," he suggested. "Maybe resting behind a stone somewhere, out of the wind? Let's check, at any rate."

He turned back into the open space of the cemetery. I followed his lead, walking around the perimeter, marked by the old stone wall, hoping to find a sleeping child but not feeling optimistic. If only I had some idea of what was going on in that wee lassie's head!

Nor did I find the bairn. What I did find, though, caused me some alarm.

At first, I thought it was just something blown in the wind from somewhere else – washing whisked off a line in Storhaven by the gales we are so used to, or dropped on the moors by a *bondi* at his work, and tumbled over and over until the stone wall stopped it. I bent to pick it up – a scarf, the sort that football fans wear. A blue and white scarf, a scarf I had seen somewhere before.

"Lyle!" I called. "Lyle, look!"

He strode over to me and took the item from my hands. He turned on the torch on his phone to look at it more closely. Then he turned the light off again and sighed.

"It's Jarvis's," he said. "You know, Jarvis from the refugee camp? The one who betrayed us to the *harkrav*. One of the only two people from the old airport who haven't come into the town. Nobody knows where he is, or what he's been doing... but he's been up here, that's for sure."

I didn't want to think it. "Not necessarily!" I said, rather desperately. "Things get blown all over this island, you know that! Don't you remember the time that Sigrid's daughter lost her swimming costume walking up from the beach, and it turned up on the shop roof in Hus?"

It was as if Lyle hadn't heard me.

"Marigold's frightened of Jarvis. Didn't you mention that, at the *fi'ilsted*, the day that we agreed to renovate the Stewart's bothy? Or was it Malcolm who told me?"

"It could have been me," I agreed. "Marigold did tell me that she was scared of him. I'm not sure if any of the other refugees liked him either."

"Was he violent?" Lyle wanted to know.

"Just strange, I think," I told him. "Rather aggressive in his manner. A bit of a loner. He tried to rescue Lavender from the sea, so Marigold told me. He stopped Marigold being swept out by the waves too, so there must be a good streak in him somewhere."

"Do you think he's unbalanced? Unpredictable?" Lyle's voice sounded tight, constrained, very controlled. "If he found her, alone up here, what would he do?" He stood looking out over the black sea. "My God!" he exclaimed. "Do you suppose he thinks that bairn owes him something? Marie," Lyle wanted to know, "do you think Jarvis would hurt Marigold?"

★★★

We phoned Tom at the ferry office, because he was coordinating things at the Storhaven end, and Sigrid in Hus. We told them that we were almost certain that Marigold had visited Lavender's grave, and we told them about Jarvis's scarf. "It's Millwall, by the way," Lyle told me. "A London football club – not famous for their polite behaviour. Do you know what they used to chant at matches? *No one likes us, we don't care!* I wish I could be sure that Marigold wasn't with him."

"I suppose Jarvis is still camping out at the old airport," I suggested. "Since he hasn't come into town."

"*Aja,*" Lyle agreed. "I suppose he is."

"Then let's go there, shall we? Just in case?"

Lyle was silent for a moment. Then, "Proper police protocol would mean I should call for backup at this point." Despite the grimness of the situation, he chuckled. "How long do you think it would take the police to come over from Lerwick?"

"Can you contact Malcolm, up on Caldbrae? The phone connection from Hus was awful, but it might be better on this side of the island…"

"Oh, *aja!*" I could hear rather than see Lyle's grin. "He would be the ideal backup!"

We should have been able to contact Malcolm, but neither of us had any success. In the end Lyle sent a text and left a message on Malcolm's answerphone, hoping that, one way or another, he would get the message.

★★★

"I seem destined to travel this road by night," I said to Lyle, when once again we were heading south towards St Matthew's Bay.

"*Aja*," agreed the *nasyoni*, sounding serious. "It's only a few months ago that you were rescuing me from those villains. You know, life was much calmer on En-Somi before your Malcolm arrived!"

"I hardly think we can blame Malcolm," I pointed out, although it was true, it had been quite an exciting winter. I had hoped that everything was settling down again now.

"Well, it won't be night much longer." Lyle nodded towards the east, where already there was a thin, grey line of light on the horizon. "It's after 4am. The sun'll be up soon."

We walked in silence for a while. The sky to the east brightened and turned from grey to gold. Over on the moors the curlews started to call, first one, and then many, their songs almost eerie in the cool morning air. Then came the clucking of fulmars from the cliffs to our right, and then the whole, unique dawn chorus of En-Somi. The rising sun made a golden path across the sea, so bright it was hard to look directly at it. Sheep started to *baa;* a small brown bird I didn't recognise sat on a rock and made little cheeping sounds. The world had woken up.

We climbed the last slope, turned the bend, and then we were peering down at the decrepit old airport buildings, looking even worse in this clean, bright morning light than they had when I had first seen them, sitting in a pony-drawn cart with Malcolm.

CHAPTER 19

"So, what now?" I asked Lyle.

"We ought to wait until Malcolm and his lot come over from Caldbrae…" he mused, but I could tell he wasn't in the mood for standing around. "God! I hope they've got our messages! But if that wee lassie is in there, with Jarvis – well, the sooner we get her out, the better!"

"*Aja.*" I had been thinking the same thing. "So, what? We just walk in, bold as brass, and see what happens?"

"I think so," Lyle agreed. "Come on!"

There was a thin wisp of smoke issuing from one of the holes in the roof of the old departure lounge.

"Well, somebody's home!" commented Lyle, as we walked down the slope towards the decaying building.

The low early-morning sun made us cast long shadows on the broken concrete where the ponies and traps used to wait in the old days, to pick up customers who had flown in. The grass on the bank was a very bright spring green, almost unreal in its freshness, sparkling a little with dew. There were dandelions and daisies growing in the gaps between rocks, and tiny yellow and white flowers which we call *frokost blomster*, literally 'breakfast flowers'. It was a beautiful morning, but I felt full of unspoken dread. If Marigold were there, what state would she be in? What could Jarvis have wanted with her? What might he have done to her? Hideous pictures filled my mind, images from films I had seen and news programmes I hadn't wanted to believe. That such terrible things could happen on En-Somi! It seemed like a nightmare.

Although Lyle had been with us when we spied on the refugees from an old sheepfold up on the moors, he had only been down here, on the ground, once before. That was after the capture of the *harkrav* villains, when the *nasyonii* and the coastguard were finishing off their work. I took the lead, walking round the building, making my way to the makeshift corrugated iron doorway.

"He'll hear us coming in," pointed out Lyle. "He'll be ready for us."

I paused. "Can we help it?" I asked.

Lyle took a deep breath. "*Nei*, we can't help it… you ought to stay out here. This is *nasyoni* business; I shouldn't be putting a civilian at risk."

"Seriously?" I was indignant. "After everything that happened on this island last winter? And anyhow, I know Marigold better than you. She trusts me."

"Humph!" Lyle was unimpressed. Of course, the bairn and her family had lived in his office until their bothy was ready. Marigold certainly knew Lyle! "Well, all right," he conceded, reluctantly. "Let's go!"

I pushed open the makeshift door, and we walked in. It took a moment for my eyes to adjust to the gloom after the bright, sunny May morning. As I did, I saw Jarvis, standing by his campfire, and behind him, held behind his back, Marigold. I thought she looked terrified.

"Good morning, Jarvis," I said, as calmly as possible. "How are you today?"

"Get out!" the man replied. "Go away! You ain't got no right to be 'ere."

"It's all right," I tried to sound relaxed, the way I thought Malcolm would. "We don't mean you any harm!"

"'O sent you 'ere? Why is you 'ere? Did that woman call you? 'Er with the blue coat? We don't want you 'ere!"

Lyle was right behind me. "Maybe not," he agreed, "but I'm *nasyoni* – police – and I have reasons to be here! Why don't you let that child go and come quietly with me? I'm sure we can sort everything out."

"I don't know 'o you is!" Jarvis declared. "But I recognise that uniform all right! And I don't know 'er, neither! You just wants to get us off this island. You wants to send us to some camp, or some prison – same fing any'ow. You wants to put this kid in care. I knows your sort. I've known your sort all me life. Get out!"

It was, of course, possible that Jarvis had never met Lyle, and Lyle was dressed in his proper *nasyoni* uniform and looked very official. But Jarvis had seen me before, several times.

I stepped forward. "Jarvis," I said, "you know me! I came over with Malcolm, don't you remember? We brought food and clothes. And you saw me up at the *harkrav's* bothy – the bosses' house, the day they were arrested. You must remember that! I was wearing Lavender's cross…"

By now my eyes had adjusted to the gloom. I could see a look of bewilderment on the man's face, nearly panic. It was almost as if he really didn't know who I was. But there was fear there too – even terror. I couldn't make any sense of it.

I heard Marigold's voice then, a little shaky. "Jarvis, it's Marie. You 'ave met 'er before. She's kind, Jarvis. She won't 'urt nobody!"

Jarvis looked even more perplexed. He turned to the little girl who was still standing behind him, as if he were trying to shield her from something. "You doesn't understand," he told her. "I's been dealing with people like this all my life! They's all kind and friendly, and they says what they only wants the best for you, and then they takes you away from everyone what you knows and makes you live with people what 'ate you and look down on you and say, 'We likes to 'ave manners in this 'ouse!' And then they says to the social worker, 'We can't cope. 'E's too 'ard for us to deal wiv,' and then they takes you away from there, and gives you to someone else, and it's the same fing over again. Or they puts you in a place where people 'it you when nobody's looking and locks you in rooms and won't let you 'ave nofing to eat unless you says 'sorry'. And you ain't sorry, so you don't say it, and then they says you're too much work, and they locks you up with boys what 'ave done bad fings, and they 'urts you... Marigold, you can't trust 'em!" He sounded desperate, "You really can't!"

Marigold came out from behind the troubled man. And then she did a brave and a kind thing. She held his hand. "But I told you," she said, "they've built us a 'ouse – well, it's called a bothy. They ain't going to take me away from Mam and Paps."

"They will! You 'as to believe me! They will!" Jarvis was looking almost wild, and sounded even more desperate than before. "They brought us up 'ere, didn't they? Your mum and dad, and all of us, and put us in tents and told us to get on wiv it! And nobody did nofing when Tracy died! And your little sister! They just put 'er in a grave with nofing to say 'o she was. I was the only one what bovered to put them stones there, to tell people 'o that little girl was! Marigold, you seen it! You knows! That's 'ow they is! They don't care! They 'ates us!"

In the dim light I could see the perplexity on Marigold's face. I couldn't tell whether she believed Jarvis, but that what he was saying went against her own experience, or whether she was trying to work out how to convince him that Lyle and I were not bad people.

But something Jarvis had said had hit home to me. "Jarvis," I asked, "was it you who put the stones on Lavender's grave? The letter 'L' and the heart?"

"What if it were?" he answered, belligerently. "Ain't no law against it!"

Then Marigold chipped in. "Jarvis put the 'L' on the grave," she told us. "It were there when I got there last night. That's 'ow I knowed it were Lavender's grave. But it were me what put the 'eart there."

"So now that she's told you," Jarvis said, "perhaps you can go away and leave us alone? 'Cause I ain't letting you put this nipper in no 'ome! And I knows, I really knows, that once a kid runs away, like Marigold did, that's it! It'll be foster carers and social workers and police and courts, and then when you grows up, it'll be camps and prisons. That's the way it is, and you knows it!"

Lyle had stayed quiet throughout this conversation, listening but letting me take the lead. Now he spoke.

"Jarvis," he asked, "if we brought Marigold's parents over here, and you saw that she was going home with them, would you let her go? Then you'd know that she was safe."

"I wouldn't know no such fing!" he responded. "I wouldn't know what they was Marigold's mum and dad! I wouldn't know what you was going to do when I couldn't see 'er or protect 'er! It could be a trick. I bin tricked before!"

"But Jarvis," I said, "you *know* Marigold's parents! They lived here with you at the airport, for years!"

"They will 'ave changed!" Jarvis answered, sounding almost sulky. "I won't know 'em no more."

It just didn't make sense. I was beginning to think that Jarvis was unwell, that he had some sort of psychological condition. "But..." I didn't know how to argue with him, how to persuade him that Marigold would be safe with us.

It was Marigold who saved the day. "Why doesn't we 'ave a brew?" she suggested, and I noticed that she was still holding Jarvis's hand, almost as if to reassure him. "Shall I put the water on?" She grinned across the distance between the fire and Lyle and me. "It ain't proper tea, like what we drinks in Hus, it's that stuff what you and Malcolm drank wiv us, when you first came!"

"That would be great!" I agreed. "Thank you. We've been walking all night!"

"It's just them two," the bairn said to Jarvis, again, as if to calm him. "And I knows 'em. Ain't no point in getting 'et up! They's 'ere now! And you can protect me, if you needs to."

Almost reluctantly, Jarvis sat down. "Better join us, then!" he told Lyle and me. "You can't drink no tea standing over there. But I warn you, I's a fighter! You ain't taking this kid away from me!"

It was, of course, a pretty tense situation, and I couldn't work out what was going on. I had always thought that Marigold didn't like Jarvis, that when the refugees had all lived together in the old airport, she was even a little frightened of him. Now, though, she seemed almost protective of the man.

Lyle and I sat by the fire, which was hissing with damp wood, and waited for the can of water to boil. Marigold produced the mugs and added the dried leaves to the water, then stirred it for a while. Jarvis watched us suspiciously, sitting with one leg under him, the other stretched out towards the fire, the black sole of his bare foot evident.

It was strange to be sitting by a fire in the decaying airport building again. In some ways it felt so familiar; in other respects it was so odd to be sitting opposite Jarvis like that – and for Marigold to be so close but out of reach. I couldn't make the man out. All sorts of thoughts were going through my head. I had seen a documentary about British prisons and the number of men in them who should really be getting psychiatric help. I was remembering homeless people on the streets of Edinburgh when I was a student and the way some of them called out as we passed and swore if we didn't give them any change. I was thinking about the trauma that Marigold had already experienced and about Jarvis's rant and his certainty that nobody in officialdom would mean any good to him or the bairn. I was hoping that Malcolm had picked up the text or the message we had left when Lyle and I couldn't contact him by phone.

"You lost your scarf," I commented, as a way to ease the tension.

Jarvis put his hand to his neck, almost instinctively. "Yeah," he agreed. "I's 'ad it all me life, since I lived wiv me mum. Now it's gone." He looked sad. "You loses ever'fing in the end," he added. "First your family, if you 'as one, then your 'ood if it gets flooded, then any friends what you makes as you gets moved around… then you loses 'ope."

"Verity said there's always 'ope," put in Marigold, unexpectedly. "Faith, 'ope and love. That's what she said."

"Yeah," Jarvis agreed, sipping his tea. "She said that, but there ain't always 'ope, no more'n there's always love. Nobody don't love me!" Then he chuckled. "No one likes us, we don't care!" He was, I realised, repeating the Millwall chant.

"Hold on!" Lyle was leaning forward, putting down his chipped mug. "Do you know Verity?"

"She were 'ere," said Marigold. "She's just gone down to the beach."

"To say 'er prayers," added Jarvis. "'Er wiv the blue coat, she's the praying sort."

"But…" Lyle was speechless. None of this made sense at all.

"She's 'iding out," explained Marigold, seeing our confused faces. "She told me. She's got some big choices to make. She wanted to get away from everyone. She told me last night, when I got 'ere."

"So was she here all last night?" I asked, and I felt a rush of relief. I was realising that whatever had happened between Jarvis and Marigold, the bairn had been safe. Verity would never have let any harm come to her. Of course, that was assuming that Verity was there by choice. But then, I realised, she couldn't be a prisoner. She had apparently been free to go down to St Matthew's Bay to pray… and she hadn't seen the need to stay to protect the bairn. But what was Verity doing at the old airport?

I saw Lyle take out his phone. I guessed he was looking to see if there was a text from Malcolm. Surely, they must be over from Caldbrae by now? We had told them where we'd be.

"'Old up!" Jarvis leapt to his feet. "You ain't calling for no 'elp! Give us that fing!" He had jumped across the fire and grabbed Lyle by the smart collar of his uniform jacket. "'And it over!"

Lyle dropped his phone. Jarvis let go of him and grabbed it. He crossed back to Marigold and handed it to her. "Is it off?" he wanted to know.

Marigold looked at the device. A few months ago she wouldn't have known what to do with it, but she had received a quick education in mobile phones once she started school. "It's turned on," she told Jarvis. "Shall I switch it off?"

"Yeah." The man was looking frightened again, almost haunted. "They can use them things to track you," he told Marigold. "That's why I took the woman's phone – Verity. 'As you still got it?"

"*Aja*, yes." Marigold produced a second phone from her jacket pocket. "It's off – it's safe."

"More'n we are!" grumbled Jarvis and seated himself again.

CHAPTER 20

We seemed to have reached some sort of impasse. It was obvious that Jarvis wasn't going to let Marigold go, and I wasn't at all sure he would let us out of his sight, either. He was utterly convinced that nobody intended him – or the bairn – any good. Lyle had lost his phone, but I still had mine. I wasn't sure, though, of how I could safely use it or of whom to call. What would I say? That we were being held by a crazy man? Was Jarvis even crazy?

Lyle must have felt just as confused. We both resumed our tea drinking and waited to see what would happen next.

And five minutes or so later, a really good thing happened.

The corrugated iron door creaked; then we heard it scratching on the concrete floor, and in came Verity.

"Morning, Jarvis and Marigold!" she called out. "It's only me, Verity, back from the beach!" Then she must have seen us. "Oh, wow!" she said, sounding cheerful and pleased to see us. "*Morgoni*, Lyle! *Morgoni*, Marie!"

Lyle jumped to his feet. "Verity!" he exclaimed. "Are you all right? Did he hurt you? Where have you been? I've been so worried! I thought you'd left the island! I thought I'd never see you again!"

Verity laughed. "Oh Lyle!" she declared. "You are so sweet! I just had to get away for a few days! I needed to do some thinking. And praying. I thought this would be a good place to hide out. I didn't know Jarvis still lived here, but he made me welcome." She grinned at Jarvis. "Well, he did once he got used to the idea of me being here! You've been good to me, haven't you, Jarvis? Cooking me fish, fresh from the sea, and then bringing young Marigold!"

Jarvis was standing too, glowering at us all. "Does you know these two?" he asked. "Marigold says she do, but one's the fuzz and I doesn't know the other."

"She was wearing her winter jacket, last time you saw her," Verity explained. "Navy-blue, with a sheepskin-lined hood. Then she wore a grey coat that Rose or someone lent her. And you noticed that she was wearing Lavender's cross."

"Oh, well – maybe," Jarvis said. For a moment I thought he looked ashamed. "There was a lot of people around then!"

Verity strolled over to the fire and seated herself on a piece of dirty plastic, next to Marigold. "I've done my thinking," she said, talking to the bairn. "I think I'll go home now. Would you like to come with me? Your mum and dad'll be worried about you."

Jarvis seemed to stiffen. "She ain't going nowhere!" he declared.

"Well…" Verity seemed very calm. "Do you plan to raise Marigold here? I mean, I suppose you could. Mo and Quincy pretty much grew up out here, didn't they? But I'm not sure it was all that good for them. And, you know, Marigold's got friends over in Hus – across the island. It doesn't seem fair to keep her away from them."

That seemed to touch a raw nerve. Jarvis looked stricken. "Is that right?" he asked the bairn. "You got friends 'ere? Kids what you 'ang out with?"

Marigold reached out to Jarvis and held his hand while she answered. "I 'ave," she told him. "Andy, 'e's the youngest in 'is family, and 'e don't go to school because 'e 'as episodes. 'E's ill, sort of. And Alana, she goes on the ferry with Duncan, and Duncan, 'e's my very best friend. And there's kids at school, but they don't understand. But they's nice. Just a bit… islandy!"

Jarvis looked thoughtful. "I 'ated them taking me away from my friends," he said. "They said it were for the best, because of the stealing and that, but they was *my* friends. I never did see 'em again. I don't want that to 'appen to you."

"It won't happen to Marigold," Verity declared. "I give you my word."

"And you's a vicar," Jarvis said. "So you 'as to tell the truth!"

"Well, not for much longer," Verity answered him. Then, "Is there any more tea in that can?"

★★★

When Malcolm, Holti, Si and Shawn burst into the derelict departure hall, about ten minutes later, it was to find a very convivial sight. I'm sure it was the last thing they expected to see – a small group sitting round the fire, drinking a concoction that passed for tea and laughing at something Marigold had been told at school: 'Why couldn't the pony sing a lullaby? Because she was a little horse!' Marigold obviously thought it was hilariously funny, and the rest of us were laughing partly because Marigold was giggling so much.

We all turned our heads, of course, as the newcomers clattered in, but only Jarvis stood, a look of alarm on his face, his fists clenched.

"Steady!" called out Lyle. "Jarvis, it's all right. Don't you see, it's Si, Marigold's dad. And Shawn. You know Shawn!"

Then Marigold saw her father and leapt to her feet. Before Jarvis could stop her, she had jumped over the fire, squeezed between Lyle and me and thrown herself into the arms of her paps. "Dad! Dad!" she said. "You came! Jarvis said what they would take me away from you, because I ran away. But I didn't run away! I just came over 'ere to find Lavender's grave! They won't take me away, will they?"

Si was holding his daughter hard, hugging her against him.

171

"Over my dead body!" he exclaimed. "Your mum and me, we won't never let nobody take you away!"

Jarvis was still standing, but there was a look of recognition on his face. "Si?" he asked, a little uncertainly.

"'Ello, mate!" Si seemed unperturbed to see Jarvis standing there. "I's been so worried about Marigold. The 'ole island's been out searching for 'er." Then, to Marigold, "Your mum's bin worried sick!"

I was looking across at Malcolm. He had his phone out and was obviously trying to make a call.

"There's no reception in here," he said, looking at me. "I'm going to let Sigrid and Tom know – we can call the search off now."

Jarvis sat down again. He looked dejected. "You's going to take the kid away!" He wasn't objecting – it was more as if he were recognising the sad reality of it. "And that police bloke will report it all to 'is boss, and you," – he pointed angrily at Si, "you won't 'ave a 'ope in 'ell if they decides you don't look after 'er properly!"

"But he does look after her properly!" Lyle objected. "He's a great father. Anyone can see that!"

Verity reached across and touched Jarvis's shoulder. "You could visit the bairn, you know. This is a small island – you can walk right across it in a day, if you want to. Less than a day, in fact. You can see for yourself that Marigold's all right."

Marigold was standing next to her paps by then, his arm round her shoulder, a grin on her face. "I'll make you some real tea!" she told Jarvis. "Not like 'ere. We've got a kettle and a' oven and three mugs what match and teaspoons what you use if you wants to put in sugar!"

"Well, fanks." Jarvis suddenly looked smaller and greyer now that the old departure hall was buzzing with people in our brightly coloured summer jackets. "But I's all right 'ere. I weren't never no good wiv people."

Malcolm came back into the shabby building. "There's mass rejoicing!" he told us. "Marigold, we need to get you back to your mam. She's worried in case you haven't had any breakfast, and Thistle's missing you!"

"Perhaps we should all be going?" suggested Si.

Verity was looking at Jarvis, huddled by his dying fire. "Jarvis," she wanted to know, "will you be all right? Do you want to come with us? Lots of the other refugees are sleeping in the kirk. You know them – they were all here, with you. And then we could find you somewhere to live – somewhere better than this."

But Jarvis wasn't interested. "I's good 'ere," he muttered. "I's got spuds and fish and this 'ere tea, and ain't nobody 'ere to bover me." Then he looked up, glowering, at Lyle. "As long as you don't 'and that kid over to them social workers! And as long as you keeps your lot away from me! Don't want no fuzz 'ere, blaming me every time somefink goes wrong on this island!"

"That seems fair enough," remarked Lyle.

"But maybe we can make the odd social visit?" asked Verity. "Just to have a cup of tea and maybe tell you the news – how Marigold's getting on, that sort of thing?"

Jarvis looked thoughtful. "Well, yeah..." he agreed. Then he added, "Wear that blue coat!"

"Right you are!" Verity seemed unfazed by this strange request.

173

CHAPTER 21

We were a merry bunch, walking to Storhaven. The sun was shining still, although the wind was up, blowing from the south, seeming to push us home. Malcolm came over to me once we had left the building.

"That could have turned out much worse!" he commented, giving me a hug.

Shawn was walking alongside Si and Marigold, just ahead of us. The two youngsters were telling each other about their adventures.

"And I couldn't ask nobody where the cemetery was," Marigold was saying, "in case they asked me 'o I was and what I was doing, but I remembered once what Duncan said it were over beyond the town, so I just walked. And it got dark, and I were lonely, but I thought what Lavender's spirit would lead me. Then I found the turning, and it were marked, and I can read now, so I followed the path, and I seen the gravestones, and I knowed I was there."

"Wasn't you scared? In a graveyard, at night?" Shawn was several years older than Marigold but clearly impressed.

Marigold reached out for her paps' hand but kept chatting to Shawn.

"I were a bit," she said. "But I thought, well, if Lavender were there, she'd look after me. And there was all these stones – you know, gravestones. And some looked really old, like 'undreds and 'undreds of years old, and a wonky cross. Then I found where Lavender were buried, and I knew it were 'er grave, because it 'ad a letter L on it, and I sat on the ground next to 'er, and I told 'er ever'thing."

"Do you fink she could 'ear you?" Shawn was fascinated, if a little doubtful.

"Oh, yeah, of course!" Marigold's certainty was impressive. "But Jarvis, 'e 'eard me too, and 'e climbs over the wall from the cliff and scares the living daylights out o' me, and 'e says to me, 'Marigold?' like in a question. Like 'e 'adn't known me all me life!"

"Yeah," Shawn agreed. "'E always does that. He asks 'o you is before 'e talks to you. My dad says it's just 'is way. Dad says it's most likely because he were shoved from pillar to post when 'e were a nipper."

"Well, I were a bit frightened because Jarvis... you know, 'e's sort of odd and I doesn't know if 'e really likes me... so then I tells 'im that I came over the island on my own, to find Lavender, and 'e were really kind, and not scary like 'e usually is. And 'e tells me that weren't a good plan, but it's done now. And 'e 'elped me collect stones to make a 'eart on Lavender's grave, because she ain't got no stone to mark where she's buried, and people might fink what nobody loved 'er. But I loved 'er. And Mam and Paps and Thistle loved 'er... then Jarvis said to go back to the old airport for the night, because it weren't right for a kid to be out alone in the dark. And Verity were there. And we 'ad fried fish and spuds and it weren't as good as at the *fi'ilsted*, but it were quite good. And I slept right next to Verity, down where Mo and Quincey used to sleep, and Verity talked in 'er sleep!"

"You wouldn't think what a vicar would talk in 'er sleep, would you?" ruminated Shawn. "You'd think what she'd be all peaceful!"

Verity and Lyle were walking behind us. At one point I turned, to check if they were still with us. They had fallen back a bit, behind the straggle of walkers, and they were holding hands, engrossed in a conversation.

"That looks promising," I said to Malcolm, nudging him and looking over my shoulder at the young couple.

Malcolm looked too and then grinned. "Love will find a way!" he remarked.

★★★

As we passed the first Storhaven bothy, and as old Mrs McNab came out to say how pleased she was that Marigold had been found, Verity and Lyle caught us up.

"*Hei*, everyone!" Lyle was trying to get our attention.

We all stopped in our tracks and then, seeing Verity's face, we gathered round, tired but happy.

Lyle and Verity were grinning. "We've got some news," Lyle announced, holding tightly to Verity's hand.

"Oh, let me guess!" muttered Malcolm to me, under his breath, and smiled.

I think Lyle heard. "You're right!" he continued. "Verity and I are going to get married!"

"Yippee!" called out Marigold. "Can I be a bridesmaid?"

EPILOGUE

It was a June wedding. Verity had resigned from the kirk. It seemed that the friendly moderator had understood her qualms, and anyhow, some of the *harkrav* congregation were unhappy about having her as their minister. She had certainly upset their peace and the steady rhythms of their lives! Neither she nor Lyle wanted to have the religious ceremony over in Storhaven, when so many of their friends lived in and around Gamla Hus. They did the legal bit at the town office, of course, with the temporary *nasyoni* officer over from Shetland doubling as registrar, but Verity and Lyle designed their own ceremony. A group of us cleared out the ruin next to Bothan Ros, because it was larger than any of our bothies, and simple, and we sat and stood in silence, while the wind whistled through the cracks in the walls and the tumble down chimney, and two pigeons roosting in the rafters cooed. A few of us wished them well, as if we were blessing them. And, naturally, Marigold was a bridesmaid and wore the first dress I had seen her in, and was as proud as punch. But none of the *harkrav* attended although Verity had invited her whole congregation, and we saw nothing of Jarvis, although Verity had been over to St Matthew's Bay specifically to tell him how welcome he'd be.

The reception, of course, was in the *fi'ilsted* and lasted way into the early hours of the morning. There was a video call from Kilmarnock involving most of Verity's extended family and a lot of toasting and singing and a few tears, because family ought to be together at times like those.

As we walked back to my bothy just after 3am, watching the sky gradually lighten and the world turning from black to grey, and as a streak of pure gold appeared on the sea, way over towards Liten Stein, Malcolm stopped and said to me, "It's a good idea, don't you think, getting married?"

I hugged him and smiled. "But, Malcolm," I answered. "Why would we? Isn't life perfect as it is?"

LOCAL DIALECT

aja yes
bondi peasant. Plural *bondii*
Bothan Ros Rose Cottage
Caldbrae Cold Hill (from *cauld brae*)
cludgie loo
domstol the court of the kirk elders (as in the elders' meeting)
En-Somi Lonely Island
En-Som-fly-Kninger refugees
En-Som-in-Fedii islanders (plural)
fi'ilsted literally 'fish hearth', best translated as 'pub'. Plural *fi'ilstedi*
frokost blomster literally 'breakfast flowers'
Gamla Husmannsplass 'Old Homestead' – the village
Gamla Hus abbreviation of *Gamla Husmannsplass*
gensi a pullover jumper. Plural *gensii*
goddi morgoni good morning. Often abbreviated to *morgoni*
gronnki sengi kale beds
harkrav from *har krav pa* – elites (literally 'entitled')
hei hi or hello
huldufolk elves (literally 'hidden people')
Hus abbreviation of *Gamla Husmannsplass*
jubel Norwegian, meaning 'cheers!'
langspil zither-like musical instrument
Liten Stein Little Rock
mam mum
mori-mori grandmother
muckle scarf cormorants

nasyoni police officer. Plural *nasyonii*

nei no

Oyrod Island Council. Members of the *Oyrod* are *oyrodii*

papa (or paps) father or dad

pari-pari grandfather

pylsa the island version of hot dogs

solstice-brenni the fires lit to celebrate the winter solstice. Plural
    solstice brennii

sommy klinger corrupt and insulting form of *En-Som-fly-Kninger*
    or refugee

un-fed outsider. Plural *un-fedii*